THE SPIRIT BOX

Don't Look!

ISBN: 978-0-9839069-0-2

Cover Concept, Artwork and Design: JH Glaze
Text Edited & Layout: Susan Grimm
First Printing August 2011
Published by MostCool Media Inc.
"Make it interesting. Make it MostCool."

Proudly printed in the United States of America.

Third Edition June 2012

12 11 10 9 8 7 6 5 4 3

Dedicated to my wife Susan, without whose support and sacrifice I may have never gotten this first book completed. Her patience with me extended to sitting for hours in coffee shops and restaurants while I cranked out parts of this story. I also wish to thank her for her many hours of final editing to iron out the rough edges.

To my Mother, who always believed in me, protected me, and loved me no matter what, but never got to see this dream be reality.

Thank you to my son, Ian, whose skill and imagination in pottery created the original box that was the inspiration for this story.

Finally, thank you to Zack Parris, my first pass editor, and my story review team: Jennifer Fakkas, James Swearengin (ISSO Productions), and others who took a chance on my first work of fiction.

The Spirit Box

"Indeed, man wishes to be happy even when he so lives as to make happiness impossible."

Saint Augustine

Prologue

The woman stood outside the shop peering through the smoky glass at the antique objects displayed on the low racks just inside the window. She debated whether to turn and walk away or follow the growing urge to go inside and browse. She hesitated, knowing well that if she walked through that door, she would ultimately find some irresistible treasure. It most certainly would be something she could not afford. Her husband would be furious if she invested too much of their money in some 'old thing' as he referred to even her most cherished antiques.

After a few moments, she lost her resolve and any rational thought was blown away by the breeze that ruffled her hair. Somehow she forgot about the look of contempt that would undoubtedly pass over her husband's face and the ugly words he would shout at her when the treasure was discovered. She stepped through the stained glass door, the small bell dangling there, ringing cheerfully behind her as she entered the well-appointed shop.

She walked around peering intently at all of the unusual items the shop contained. Through the window from the outside, the shop had appeared to be quite large, but now she realized it was an illusion. Various crates were stacked to display curios and small decorative on them, shelves were near overflowing, and it gave her a feeling of claustrophobia to be moving around in such a tight space.

She was examining some old dishes, elaborate pots and intricately carved wooden boxes, when a slightly disheveled looking man came to the counter from a room in the back. Though the doorway was hung with a curtain of beads, it hardly made a sound as he parted them. Her back was facing him, and he quietly greeted her so as not to startle her. "Guten tag."

She turned to look at him with some confusion and replied, "I'm sorry, do you speak English?"

"Ah, English, yes, and where are you from, madam?" He forced half a smile, but she could tell from looking into his reddened eyes that something was troubling the older man as he crossed his arms and awaited her response.

"Well, sir, I am from the U. S. and my husband and I are here to celebrate our wedding anniversary."

The old man judged her to be about as happy as she judged him to be. "Very good, and you are looking for a gift? Have you been married long?"

He seemed to be genuinely interested in the answer to this question, so she told him. "Twenty years this month. I wish I could say it's been blissful, but we can't have everything we wish for, now can we?" She looked down at the counter that separated them as she spoke, a deep sadness falling over her.

He hesitated, "And what is it you would wish for, Miss, if you could have anything you wanted?" He was wearing wire-framed glasses and he pushed them up further on his nose as he asked the question.

"Oh... I would love to have a little shop like this, and... to be happy I guess. But then I think a small shop with all of these treasures could help me to feel happy again." Her face brightened as she told him her dreams. "And if my husband understood me better, I guess that would help too." She turned her head slightly now trying to avert her eyes in case tears might start flowing. She was feeling the weight of her words as she spoke them.

"And you would have a shop like this if you could?" He leaned on the glass counter with palms down, and positioned himself better to see into her eyes.

"Oh, I've always dreamt of it! I have a very small collection of antique items and, if I had it such a place, I'd be able to surround myself all the more with such lovely things." Such a simple statement, yet the sound of hope began to return to her voice.

"And what if I told you it is very easy to have your shop and anything else you desire for that matter." He stood upright again as her shimmering eyes turned toward him.

"Either I would say you were mad, or I would ask how it is possible. Of course, you must realize I don't have the money to open a shop. In the U.S., the rent on the building alone would be very expensive, I'm afraid."

"Ah, yes... the money. I have an answer for you in the back room, but you must promise never to tell anyone." He started to turn to walk back through the beaded curtain doorway

"Excuse me, sir, an answer in the back room? Oh, I'm sorry you must have misunderstood! I could never do…"

"No madam, you misunderstand. Of course, I am not asking you to go along to the back room. Please, just wait here for a moment. I have a very special item to show you. It is very ancient and I think you will have a great interest in it from what you have told me." With that he turned and hurried into the back room. A moment later he reappeared carrying a cube-shaped wooden box. As he sat it on the counter, she saw that it was made from a beautiful dark wood she had never seen before. Richly grained, it was unlike anything she had ever seen.

"Madam, I would like you to consider this item. The wooden box is very special, but it is the box within the box that is truly a magical piece." He framed the box with his long bony fingers as he spoke.

"It is a very beautiful box, but you say there is another box inside of this one? Why would you put a box inside of a box? And why are there so many screws around the edge, surely it wouldn't take so many to hold the box together."

"No, it would not take so many if this was your typical antique box, but this box is constructed in a very special way to protect its very special contents. I call it a Spirit Box though it has gone by other names over the centuries."

"Centuries? How old is it?" she touched the wood and felt a warmth in her fingertips as she ran them over the surface. "It feels warm to the touch."

"Sometimes it feels warm, and other times it is cooler than the temperature of the room. Hidden inside is the treasure you seek, the one that can give you anything you desire."

"Oh please, sir, don't take me for a fool!" She looked at him as if he were telling her a wild tale. She had no idea that the wild tale had just begun.

"If you have a bit of time, I will tell you the story of this box, but you must promise me that you will buy it from me and take it with you when you return to your home and never return it to this store." He scratched his balding head and watched her formulate her answer.

"How can I promise to buy it when you have not even mentioned the price?"

"Oh, I am sorry. For you, right now, today, you can have this wonderful piece for only twenty-five U.S. dollars. It is a very reasonable price even for the outer box, would you not agree?" He mustered up his best salesman smile, but inside he was holding his breath.

"Yes, that is a very good price for such a fine piece, but if it is all that you say, why would you make such a deal?" She looked the shopkeeper square in the eye.

"Madam, this box belonged to my wife who recently died. It makes me very sad to have it here. I must sell it no matter the cost in order to recover from this terrible loss." He could not look her in the eye, but sadly bowed his head shaking it from side to side.

She turned away from the counter, looking around the store for a moment. "Will it really help me to have my own store?"

"Oh yes, and anything else you desire. That is something you can decide for yourself, how you will use it, when you return home."

"Can I see the other box, this Spirit Box? After all, I would not want to take it and find out as I am going through Customs that you tricked me into smuggling drugs for you." She wanted to get a look at the box that was said to be so special. Obviously, the man was prone to melodrama and wild exaggerations, but she was intrigued.

"First you must make the promise I have asked. It is a promise you cannot refuse once you have made it." He waited for her response, willing her to agree to his terms.

"Yes, yes. If there is another box inside of this box, I promise to do what you have asked, and I will never bring it back to this place."

Now the shopkeeper smiled wide enough to expose his yellow teeth and reached beneath the counter to produce a small screwdriver, which he used to quickly remove the screws from one side of the box. He carefully lifted the panel away and revealed the well-packed contents. She could see four small spike-like extensions from what appeared to be the lid of the pottery box within. She reached down and pulled it partially from the container to reveal the lid was in the shape of a crown.

"Please, be careful! Do not remove it!" The man looked quite distressed.

Seeing the side of the box, she realized that there was a face, an old looking face carved into it, and she became very excited. It was much more beautiful than she had imagined, and must be quite valuable. She eased it back into its packing and, when her hands were clear, the shopkeeper quickly placed the panel back into position and drove the screws back into place.

When he was finished, he looked up at her and held out his hand. "Twenty-five dollars, please."

Looking down at his hand, the woman spoke as she opened her purse. "Before I take it, can you tell me where this unusual box comes from? I may need to sell it myself one day, and it would help if I knew some of its history."

"Yes, it will come to you with quite a history. Now that you have promised to take the Spirit Box, it will not allow you to leave without it. I can tell you its story, although the box can relate its tale better than I. I will begin the tale, and perhaps the box will take over and save me the trouble. Please place your hand on the top of the box and close your eyes."

"Why do I need to do that?" She was losing patience with the shopkeeper's story. On the other hand, if what he said was true, then... involuntarily she moved away from the counter.

"Don't be afraid, madam, the box cannot hurt you for you are now its keeper. However, if you do as I say you may actually 'see' the story as I tell it. As I said, it is a very unique piece and the story, well, when you see it, you will believe it." He took her hand, which was shaking a bit now and she wondered what she had gotten herself into. Gently, the old man placed her hand on top of the box. "Now just close your eyes," he said, and she did. He began to speak, but his voice sounded somewhat different, maybe deeper, maybe older, she couldn't tell, and the story began.

Around the fifth century A.D., Nordic clans known as the Krag ruled the land from the rock-lined shores of the cold, dark sea to the highest heights of the snow-tipped peaks where none had ever succeeded to make the climb. The king of the Krag was just as cold and forbidding as the land he ruled. He was called Torakel, a large scarred hulk of a man, a fierce warrior who ruled his people by the axe, bone and blood. Torakel's word was Law, and no one dared to defy him for his vengeance was swift and certain.

One bitter spring morning, while the Krag were preoccupied preparing for the long hunt, Hun invaders entered the land from the Northern shores, their terrifying masses gathering on the plains. Archer's arrows rained down upon the Krag, blackening the sky with a sound like the howling wind. Many of Torakel's men fell that morning with bolts through their arms, necks, and their heads as their shields could not stop the constant bombardment and became shattered from the damage inflicted upon them.

With her eyes closed, she could see the battle as if it was here in front of her, or maybe she was there. It was as though she were actually present on the day of the battle for she could hear the carnage and smell the stench of blood and death. She tried to open her eyes but she could see the shop no longer. She could not escape the battlefield.

Those who withstood the plunging arrows were met with fireballs and giant stones hurtled across the battlefield by crudely built catapults and from these projectiles, there was no real defense. The fighting lasted for days and thousands of Krag and their enemy alike were slaughtered, leaving piles of dead bodies scattered across the plain.

Fate was present at the battle on the third day and, as the sun rose high in the sky, an archer's arrow fell from the clouds and struck Torakel in the small gap between his neck and the armored leather breast plate that had so many times before saved his life in battle. The arrow hit hard in the shoulder, piercing his flesh cutting deep and slicing through sinew and artery. Torakel was fading quickly as his lifeblood spurted from the wound.

Seeing their mighty king fall, clansmen fighting nearby rushed to his side to protect and assist, but soon realized that there was nothing they could do to save him. Torakel looked at his men through eyes already dim and watched them shake their heads and whisper in hushed frightened tones to one another. With a rasping voice, the king called for his most trusted servant to be summoned to witness his final wishes and to prepare his body for the journey home.

The battle around them was thinning as the last of the enemy headed back for protection in the heavy brush beneath the tall trees lining the bloody field. Torakel could sense that the battle would soon end and his kingdom would stand. Very soon two of his men reappeared with the only man in all the Krag who served the king with less fear than affection. A pained look flashed across the servant's face as he leaned close and turned his head to hear the final words of his master.

"Who is this king?" she asked, her voice echoing inside of her head. "Why do I have to witness his death? I don't want to watch this!" She closed her eyes very tightly.

The strange voice of the shopkeeper answered, "You will need to understand this time of darkness to know why you must respect the box, and its power."

With blood still trickling from the corner of his mouth and in forced painful breaths signaling the final moments of his life, Torakel spoke two requests to his trusted servant. "Tell my son and his mother the time has come to fulfill their promise of lasting love and loyalty," he gasped between breaths. "Summon Alron to perform the Ritual." As the last word passed from his lips, his head lolled to the side and he was gone.

"Is he dead?" She tried to understand how this death was part of the story of the box.

"The king was a powerful man, and he will not settle for passing from this world. He was a man of vision and he had a plan for this day."

She turned to the shopkeeper, realizing for the first time that he was in this world with her. The scene went dark before her and they were alone in the darkness.

The shopkeeper continued his story as another man appeared before them dressed in colorful robes and clothing. Now the three stood alone, but it seemed the other man could not see them. He stood looking into the blackness, lost in his loneliness.

Alron, was known to the Krag as the dark shaman, and had come from a far away land, a wanderer, a man of deception and half-truths. He brought with him dark secrets and magical powers offered to Torakel to assist in the destruction of their enemies. The black powder the mysterious shaman had brought from the East had given the Krag a decisive edge on the battlefield and with astonishing visions and premonitions of battles Alron advised and manipulated his new king.

In truth, the visions of Alron were no more than strategies he had learned while in combat, and as a servant to his former master who had died with his people during a great war. Alron had an overwhelming lust for power and had seen how the holy men were revered in his homeland. When he found that he had escaped the carnage of the battle that destroyed his people, he carried away with him the rich dark robes of the dead shaman who had been slain along with the others.

Suffering grim and inhospitable conditions, Alron traveled northward with single-minded ambition. When he finally chanced upon the Krag, he overcame their suspicions with the appearance of humility presenting himself as a holy man from the East who had heard the voices of gods. The very gods themselves had summoned him to the land of the Krag to assist them in their quest for greater territory and treasure.

Until the moment of Torakel's dying request, the Ritual of the Spirit Box had been told for many years as the story of Soronna. The story, now a legend, was nothing more than a concocted tale of resurrection and power that Alron had used to win the position of High Shaman among the clan.   Each time the story was told it was embellished with just enough detail to enthrall the audience and elevate the status of the only one that could tell it.

"So this Alron was a con man?" She was trying to make sense of the story, but the heavily robed man did not appear to be someone who could perform magic ceremonies. "The Soronna was his con? How could they believe such a wild tale?"

The shopkeeper stepped toward the vision of Alron, "There was magic in those times, which even the shaman was not aware."

The elaborate legend was always recounted in hushed foreboding tones, and only in the presence of Torakel and his servants. Thus, there was no one to challenge his wild fantasy that a box made of clay pottery could carry a spirit to eternal life.

Now the High Shaman would be asked to actually perform a ceremony that did not truly exist except in his imagination. A powerful imagination it was, and Alron did not find it difficult to dream up vivid details spoken in the colorful language and tone of a great holy man. Bringing the legend to life was something different however.

The story of Soronna included the plans for construction of the Spirit Box:

Now the two onlookers were standing in a building with a fiery kiln and there was a man working with clay on a table. He was forming a box with what appeared to be a human face, and the potter was adding detail to the features of the face.

"The box shall be constructed of sacred clay, the substance used by the gods in the creation of life. It shall be one and a half hands high and the clay shall be mixed with the blood of a sacrificed goat and the ashes of an incinerated crow."

"This box shall bear four sides, and on one, the face of the king whose Spirit would dwell inside until the time of the gathering of spirits allow the resurrection of the body in an infant child."

"The eyes of the face on the box shall be open to allow the Spirit inside to see the world around it while it awaited the rebirth. The mouth shall include a tongue for speaking, but this tongue must be hidden so that the servant of the box alone can hear the bidding of the Spirit."

"The lid of the box shall be made in the shape of the king's crown and placed on the box to contain the Spirit within. It should be inlaid with gold and fitted tightly to prevent the weak from opening the box."

Alron had told his new people that upon the death of the king a ceremony was to be held. During this ceremony, the heart of the fallen leader would be removed, revived, and placed in the box where it would reside until one hundred lesser spirits, collected through the assistance of a willing servant, empowered its release and reincarnation.

Years before this fateful day, servants of the king had constructed the Spirit Box of dark clay, sacrificial blood, and ash. The facial features of Torakel had been carved into the front of the box just as the legend had instructed. The likeness to the living ruler was remarkable and haunting. So lifelike in fact was the face of the king on the box, that when an observer moved within the room where it sat displayed upon a specially carved table, it's lifeless eyes seemed to follow.

Now, after these long years the time had come. Alron was called and compelled to prepare the ceremony.

"So now the king is dead, and this shaman is going to put the heart of the king in the box to collect spirits?" she asked the shopkeeper who was now looking very tired as he stood facing her.

"Yes, it was his destiny that one day he would have to follow through with his scheme, and now he is fearful that his lies will all be revealed and the people will kill him in their anguish and anger."

For the first time since coming to the Krag, Alron was at a loss. What was the ceremony? A lie had been created to increase his standing among the clan and its leader. Magic was expected that did not exist. His lies were about to be exposed and he would surely be torn apart by an angry mob of expectant clansmen.

Alron responded to the king's request for the ritual by demanding an hour of silent reflection with his lord and master. A burial preparation hut was used to prepare the bodies of the dead for burial and the king's body had been laid upon a large wooden table. He had been washed and wrapped in linen, leaving nothing exposed but the area surrounding the king's heart.

Inside the large hut, Alron sat on a stool beside Torakel's body, his face in his hands. His sense of dread heightened with each passing moment, the sweat beginning to drip from his forehead into his fingers. Aware that he was closer to his own bloody end at the hands of his adopted people, Alron cried out to the gods he did not believe existed.

He studied Torakel for a long moment, wondering how to perform this imaginary ritual. What could he do that would satisfy the mourning people waiting outside?

As he sat staring at the lifeless body, he had a vision - a ring of burning torches, young virgins standing between each torch, and the wife and son of the king completing the circle in front of the box. The body of the lifeless leader should be placed on a broad table set upon a pyre. On a smaller platform, just below and in front of the body should be placed the Spirit Box.

As darkness was but two hours away, Alron went out from the hut and commanded that the ceremonial site be prepared. He directed the king's servants to build the site just as he had seen in his vision. He warned them to work quickly, threatening them with certain death if they failed.

Now the woman and shopkeeper were standing at the clearing as villagers worked quickly as their lives depended on it. The woman made a face of discomfort as occasionally a villager would pass through her as if she were nothing but mist.

"What are they thinking? This surely will come to a bad end, why don't they just burn the body?'

"The shaman has made a covenant with the king and his people. Not fulfilling this promise would mean certain death. He has no choice but to follow through with it."

Torches were brought into the selected clearing, six in all, and placed in the ground forming a circle. Strongmen carried logs taken from the village huts and piled them in the center of the ring. A broad tabletop was carried from Torakel's home and was placed on the top of the pile. Then the Spirit Box was placed in front of the pile on a smaller table.

As darkness fell, large fires were built around the perimeter for light. Warriors took their places at the outer edge to guard against any enemy who dared to return. The torches were lit and Torakel's body was carried and placed on the table. The clan was called to assemble, and Torakel's wife and son took their place at the front of the great procession leading to the site.

Alron carefully timed his arrival, dressed in his finest ceremonial robes. A look of deep concern lined his face for he still did not know the words he would say. To the crowd assembling there, it appeared that he was deep in reverent concentration. Soon the leader of the people, mighty Torakel, would be sent on a final journey toward eternal life.

Alron trembled in the shadows of the torchlight, fearing that the time had come when the biggest deception of his life as the Krag's High Shaman was about to be revealed. Finally, Alron took a deep breath and stepped forward. He turned to face the village and spoke.

"The mighty Torakel has requested that his beloved and faithful people be present for the Soronna ceremony. Please come now and take your place in the circle of light. Six young virgins have been chosen, the youngest of these shall be six years old and each of the others shall be six months older than the one before as the ritual prescribes."

Alron turned to girls dressed in ceremonial white shimmering in the light of the torches. "Come now and stand with me between the torches and the family of our lord at my side."

Six young girls stepped one at a time to their places. Torakel's wife and son stepped to the side of the large table, and the circle was complete just as Alron had envisioned.

The High Shaman raised his hands and, turning his face to the sky, began to speak. He began with a familiar chant common to the people, asking for the blessings of the gods for their lives, their crops, and their safety. As he spoke, Alron closed his eyes and felt a warm sensation spreading throughout his body.

The shaman, startled by this feeling, paused with arms stretched above his head. For a moment, he found that he could not speak and even as he moved his mouth, no words could escape it.

Suddenly his head jerked back and he felt something dark and cold taking control of his body, something ancient and hungry.

Then the words came.

Coming up from the bottom of his stomach, Alron could feel them as they moved up his esophagus, like a warm glob of congealed animal fat to his throat, to his now paralyzed lips. Though his mouth was open and unmoving, the words began to spill from it.

He spoke in a voice that was not from this world and it sprang forth loudly as if backed by thunder.

"Ar ala de magresh tran da!"

Lightning struck a nearby tree and the shock sent terror spreading up from his feet and revealed itself on Alron's face as he realized he could not control what he was saying.

The words came faster now.

"Movoron intlecti si octohan!"

As the strange chant echoed across the clearing, the people assembled around him saw the clouds above them begin to move, spiraling slowly at first, with bursts of lightning and flashes of blue illuminating from within.

Alron felt his body begin to move. He was unable to move, but his body took each step on its own, moving him closer to the table where the Spirit Box had been placed, a sharp dagger at the right of it.

Alron's arm moved with such force he could do nothing to stop it, his hand grasping the handle of the dagger. He tried to scream out, but the only sound that could escape his paralyzed lips were the words that continued to rise from the depths of his bowels. He was beginning to feel as though his very life was being drained from his body and was being replaced by a scorching fire as the clouds continued to spiral lower and hovered now just above the broad table.

He was helpless to stop it.

With one terrible stroke, the horrified shaman raised the dagger high and thrust the long blade into the chest of Torakel just below the base of his neck. The sound of cracking bone was barely audible above the roar of the wind that had blown in with the swirling clouds.

The crowd gasped at the small river of black blood flowed from the wound and the dagger was plunged again and again, opening the chest to reveal the lifeless heart of the king.

When enough of the bone, muscle and cartilage had been cut away, the blade dropped from Alron's hand, which plunged deep into Torakel's chest, ripping the heart from it's home of forty-plus years, separating arteries and veins and spraying blood into Alron's open gasping mouth.

He wished he could vomit as the cold sticky fluid began to run down the back of his throat, but still he could not stop the words that spilled from his lips long enough to manage even a gag.

A bolt of lightning came from the clouds, and as the dead heart was held high over the table above the Spirit Box, it struck with a thunderous crash.

The cold piece of flesh in the shaman's hand now began to throb and twitch. The black fluid oozing from the heart began to shine, crimson with life, now flowing down the arm that held it up for all to see.

Alron could only watch from inside his own traitorous body as it moved closer to the table and removed the lid from the box, placing it carefully on the table.

Gingerly the heart was placed in the box, and Alron felt himself taking one step backward. The tirade of chanting from his throat grew louder and louder and then suddenly all noise and motion stopped. Silence fell upon the clearing.

The clan folk were speechless. Not one of them had ever witnessed anything like this before, and though they wished to run screaming from the clearing, their legs had become wooden and unable to move.

Suddenly, a single bolt of swirling lightning came from the clouds and struck straight inside of the Spirit Box illuminating the heart with a blue light. As the clan watched in horror, Alron's mouth began to open even wider. The mouths of the frightened girls in the circle also began to open, and those of Torakel's family did the same.

Terror filled the eyes of each ceremonial participant as their mouths continued to open wider and wider making a terrible cracking noise as jaws were separated from skulls, the lower jaw of each resting against their chest. Then as if an earthquake welled up inside each one, they began to shake, though their feet held firmly to the ground. A glowing *blue light began to form in their gaping mouths, coming from their throats.*

The glowing blue light was now changing and reaching out from each of their bodies. Each light began to take on a form resembling the face, then shoulders and torso of each of the paralyzed victims. As the ghostly forms stretched away from the bodies, they were drawn toward the Spirit Box until the entire glowing shape of each victim seemed to hang from their open mouths, held there by the feet.

The flesh of each victim had shriveled as their spirits were drawn out of them. What was left appeared to be burned, or dried in an intensely rapid heat that changed their pale skin to a wrinkled brown color with a skeletal outline clearly visible beneath it.

A piercing shriek echoed through the clearing as suddenly the nine glowing spirits were ripped from the withered bodies of Alron, Torakel's family, and the six young virgins who had been gathered in the circle. With a clap of thunder and a brilliant flash, the spirits disappeared into the box. The lid then levitated and slammed on the top, sealing their fate.

The woman felt paralyzed as the terrible story came to a conclusion and though she had tried closing her eyes, even covering them with her hands, she could still see and hear every movement, every horrible vision as the people who surrounded her in this clearing, died.

Finally she could breathe again and the scream that had been held back came pouring from her lips. Suddenly she was back in the shop standing at the counter across from the shopkeeper.

"Twenty-five dollars, please. Madam, I must insist you take the box now and leave." The shopkeeper held out his hand again.

"I can't take this… this thing! What I saw was terrible and there is no way I can bring this into my home." She appeared to be very shaken.

"I am sorry madam but the box is yours whether you pay me or not. If you try to leave without, it will surely take your spirit. Please, I do not want to have to dispose of your body. Believe me when I tell you this box has the power to fulfill your dreams, it simply depends on what you are willing to do to have them."

She let out a great sigh and reached into her handbag and pulled out twenty-five dollars and handed it to the man. Then she picked up the box without a word and hurried out of the shop into the street.

The shopkeeper followed her to the door, closed and locked it, then retired to the back room of the store where the remains of his wife waited silently.

That was long ago…

One

It was 3 o'clock on Friday and people in the office were already beginning to focus on the weekend instead of the tasks at hand. Everyone, that is, except Walt Turner. Walt had a spreadsheet to finish, a special project from the boss for the evening meeting, and he was running out of time to get it finished.

"You worthless piece of shit!" came the tirade drifting from out of Walt's cubicle. "You scum sucking, lowlife, motherfuckin' piece of PC bullshit!" Walt picked up his keyboard and slammed it down with a loud clatter.

Greg eased up from his comfortable ergonomic office chair and cautiously peered over the top of the cube wall. On the other side, Walt was about to throw his laptop to the floor with the wires and external monitor still connected.

"Dude," exclaimed Greg. "Chill out man it's only a computer, you can't beat it into submission!"

Walt turned to look at him with rage in his eyes and spat back, "Oh yeah? To you it's only a computer, to me it's a motherfuckin' harpy sent by demons of the underworld to rip chunks of flesh from my 43-year old ass!"

Greg came around the cube asking, "What's the problem, bro?" Then, on Walt's still connected external monitor, he saw it, the Blue Screen of Death. The last thing anyone wanted to see as they were putting the final touches on a spreadsheet for the evening meeting of the upper management, especially on a Friday.

"Shit, man," he empathized. "What are you gonna do? Isn't that spreadsheet due by 4:30?"

"I don't know," yowled Walt with his hands pressed against his head. "I am so fucked right now I can't even think straight. Mr. Shithead Palmer said that he 'really needed' this spreadsheet for review before the Board meeting tonight. I was supposed to meet with him at 4:30 or something to review the details for final tweaks. Now I am totally hosed! I'll have to cancel on him and he is gonna be *extremely* pissed! I'll be lucky if I get out of here by 6 o'clock!"

Walt was pacing, arms gesturing wildly, "But wait, there's more! Not only did I lose *every*thing I was working on, I don't even know if this fucker'll reboot! I'm dead, man!"

Greg shook his head. "You know I feel ya, man – been there done that." What Greg was really thinking was, *Serves you right, you strange-ass fucker! It seems there is a God after all!*

"Tell you what, bro", said Greg. "Because I am such a generous good-looking guy, how 'bout you use my computer to finish your shit, and I'll just blow out of here an hour early and run some errands?"

"Hey, thanks a lot!" said Walt, "but you're forgetting I need access to the network to get to the data."

"No problemo, my friend, you can access all your data from my computer through the network, it's all there. In fact, you could do that with any computer in the building, but I wouldn't advise it. I can imagine the look on Kathie's face if she came back from the coffee room and you were sitting in her cube crankin' out a spreadsheet on her laptop. I know she'd fuckin' freak!"

"You really think she'd be pissed?" asked Walt. "I personally believe there are moments when my manly charms are beginning to break down her otherwise stone-cold bitch exterior."

"Dude, believe what you want, but the way she jumps at every sound anytime somebody walks past her cube, I can almost guarantee, THAT would freak her out," laughed Greg.

"Whatever," said Walt. "I don't exactly have the time to stand around and debate it, so is it cool for me to use your computer to get this stuff done?"

"Sure buddy, get your stuff and I'll hook you up."

"Here, take this folder and I'll get the rest of it," directed Walt, already gathering the papers that were scattered on his desk.

Greg smiled as he took the folder from Walt's hand. "Don't worry man, you'll get it all done and everything will be cool."

An hour and a half passed and the silence of the office created a buzz in Walt's ears. By now the only living creatures left in the office had to be Walt, the cubicle spiders, and those weird hairy centipedes that were so prevalent in the building.

Old Man Palmer was not too happy that Walt had cancelled the review meeting, but he told Walt that he trusted in his ability to come through. Besides, Palmer noted that Walt must surely understand how important this project was, not only to the company but also to Walt's future in it.

When Walt had been given the assignment, Palmer had used phrases like, "This could mean bigger things for you." And, "Your future here is very bright, Mr. Turner. You might start thinking about an office instead of that cubicle if things keep going so well."

Walt had lapped up those tidbits of praise and hope like a half-starved street dog. All the folks working for Palmer knew he could fire you on a whim, but Walt tried hard to keep a low profile and do his job hoping to get a promotion some day. Now an unexpected computer problem made a bright future seem like a dim prospect if the spreadsheet could not be finished in time. Walt bent his head over Greg's keyboard and got right to work.

At last, the spreadsheet was completed. Walt clicked the save button and leaned back with satisfaction. Palmer had instructed Walt to email the spreadsheet to him as soon as it was finished. He noticed with some sense of relief that the icon for Greg's email was still in the program tray at the bottom of the screen and, better than that, it was open. This meant that Walt could send the spreadsheet without delay and keep his ass out of the unemployment line for one more day. He clicked the icon for the email client and then "new message".

He typed Palmer into the "To" line and Mr. Palmer's email address appeared. In the subject line he entered, "Your Spreadsheet" and then attached the file. He began to rise from his seat with his finger still on the keyboard. He didn't notice the auto signature for Greg at the bottom of the email. At least, it didn't register in his brain before he clicked to send.

Standing now, Walt shut down Greg's computer and, after a few seconds, the screen went black and he pushed the chair against the desk. He walked around the cubicle wall and looked at his blue screen of death still shining there. Reaching down to press the power button, heard a sound from the doorway to his left. As the screen went black, he quickly closed his laptop, shoved it into his backpack and zipped it shut.

Walt stood up just in time to see Mr. Palmer walking into his office. Not wanting to be seen there, he grabbed his coat and snuck out as quietly as possible between the cubicles and slipped out the door, closing it carefully to keep it from making a sound.

Two

Hurriedly Walt walked toward the outside exit and pushed the green button on the wall to unlock the door. He moved through the doorway while putting on his coat, and crossed the parking lot. Once he made it to the sidewalk, Walt turned right to begin trekking the five blocks to his apartment.

It was dark now, and the streetlights created eerie shadows from the trees and signs that lined the street. There wasn't much traffic on this side street at this hour and he walked about a block and a half before the first car approached. Even though the car was about two blocks away he could hear the thump, thump, thump of the bass line of the song the driver was listening to.

As the car came closer, it began to slow and he saw the window opening to reveal a young man in his late teens or early twenties behind the wheel. Suddenly the car slowed next to him. The young man reached down to turn down the music and said, "Hey old man, where you goin'?"

Walt's pulse raced as he tried to ignore the guy, not making eye contact. He just kept walking with his head down and straight ahead. He had heard of situations like this and he felt it might be best to appear to be in a hurry and ignore the guy rather than give him a reason to start something.

The car stopped and he heard the car door open behind him. He sensed the young thug walking toward him, and as he came closer he yelled.

"Hey muh fucker, I axed you a question. Where you goin' in *my* hood, bitch?"

Just then Walt stopped and turned to face the young man. He reached into his pocket and paused, fingering the cold metal in his hand, then said with a smile on his face, "I'll tell you what, you fucking punk, you get back in your car and drive away..." Pulling a pistol from his pocket, Walt continued, "...and I will let your stupid ass live another day. Run your ass home now and fuck your sister. Maybe if you're quick about it, I won't put a hole in your piece o' shit car while you're leaving!"

The younger guy's mouth dropped open as he could clearly see the silver pistol in Walt's hand. As he turned and took that first step toward his car, he didn't notice the tree root pushing up the sidewalk as he tripped and fell face first to the concrete, cracking his chin against it with a loud "whack".

Walt said "OOOWWW, I bet that hurt, bitch!"

Without skipping a beat, the so-called thug was up and running toward his car. He had left the door wide open when he stopped to harass Walt, so he jumped on in, slammed the car in gear and burned rubber halfway down the block.

As Walt turned the corner, a satisfied smile spread across his face. While his mother was still alive, he would have never thought to buy a gun, let alone carry it in public. Now he thought back to the day when he had gotten that permit to carry a concealed weapon, how he had anticipated that this day would come, and although he was admittedly shaken, a sense of power came over him as the residual adrenaline spread through his body.

So this is how it feels to be the one in control. Walt thought about this as he continued walking. This is what it was like to wield power over another human being. It was a concept that he knew only from reading books or from movies, but now he was living it in the moment, and it was an enjoyable sensation.

He was two blocks from home when he realized he was somewhat hungry. The effects of his adrenaline rush were beginning to subside. Since it was later than usual, and he didn't feel much like going home to cook something for dinner, he crossed the street to the Big T Diner. He had been eating at the diner for the past couple of years ever since his mother had taken ill and was unable to cook for them.

As he stepped through the door, a grinning Big T greeted Walt.

"Hey Walt," he said. "What's shakin'?"

"S.O.S., T." Walt replied, "More work, more bills, and nobody at home to kick around when I get there, so I figured I'd come by and let you make me a burger."

"Sure thing Walt," Big T replied with a smile. "Fries with that?"

"Slaw, too" nodded Walt, taking off his coat and sliding into a booth. The dinner rush, if there had ever been one, was obviously over. The only other person in the restaurant was an apparent drunk, who was sitting slumped over a plate of pancakes.

Although obviously drunk, the man did not appear to be a down-and-out homeless drunk. As a matter of fact he was nicely dressed. As he bent toward the table in the booth, his close-cropped brown hair was merely inches from the pool of the syrup in his plate.

"Looks like somebody got an early start tonight." Walt wagged his head toward the stranger. "Seems like a waste of a great stack of cakes."

Big T replied, "That's Jerry. Wife left him last week and he's been coming in drunk every day since. Says he never learned how to cook and if it weren't for me, he'd starve to death. Course he was drunk when he said it… anyway his money's good and I kinda feel sorry for him. Besides he never comes during the busy times, so I let him chill out a minute, when he needs to."

Big T was no stranger to sorrow. He got the nickname growing up here in the neighborhood. His real name was Troy Jones, and just like his nickname indicates, he was a very large man. He inherited the diner when his father and mother were killed in a motorcycle accident out in Colorado.

At the time, he was about 25 years old and just out of prison where he served five long years for putting his girlfriend's ex-boyfriend in the hospital. Something took hold of T that night and he just lost control. The EMT who had responded when the beating was called in said he had never seen anyone beaten so severely and still alive. T barely escaped being charged with murder.

When the motorcycle accident took the life of his parents, Big T made up his mind to change his life, maybe even get married and have a family. He wanted his life to count for something besides the life he nearly took in a jealous rage.

Fortune smiled on him, and Big T's dream came true. At the age of 30, he married Janie, a waitress working at the diner. A year later Janie became pregnant, and they had a beautiful son.

But something was wrong with Janie. Happiness had evaporated from her world. The doctors had said that she was most likely suffering from post partum syndrome. They explained that her disappearances, for days at time, stemmed from the great bouts of depression she was obviously experiencing.

Great bouts of depression didn't explain it well enough. There were times when Walt had entered the diner late in the afternoon and there was Janie, screaming at T. She would be holding the baby saying, "Shit T, I can't handle this," and, "I need to get out of here for a minute and get my head together."

Then she would leave the baby on the counter in his car seat and take off down the street. Often three or four days would go by, and each time she returned, she seemed more of a shell of a person than the time before.

Big T was tortured with this for about a year. He tried to get a grip on what was happening, really he did. He had nearly accepted the fact that his life would continue to be filled with craziness, when one day Janie left and took the baby with her. When T finally figured it out, she was halfway across the state and he never saw her again.

So he could really empathize with a poor slob whose wife had just left him and taken their kid.

Walt joked, "What's up with the burger, T? Did you have to wait while the cow bled out? I mean I like fresh meat and all, but I prefer not to hear the 'moo's' while you slaughter it in the back room!" He chuckled a little too loudly at his own joke.

Walt had a way of joking with people that most took to be rather rude, if not downright strange. He would start out with something that could be considered funny, then take it to the next level with such a sharply defined description that it could no longer be taken as a joke.

How many friends do you have now, Walt? The voice came from inside of Walt's head, or did it? He glanced around but no one was there.

Big T looked up over the counter where he was preparing the burger and yelled over the noise to Walt, "Dude did you say something? This fan back here is loud as shit and the only thing I can hear is the bell that rings when the door opens. In fact, before I got that bell, I was going broke from the homeless people sliding in here and eating the pie and donuts that sit out there on the counter."

As he spoke, he pointed at the tall metal stand inside the glass-walled cooler. Inside were all of the pies and donuts, carefully arranged to make someone hungry when all they came in for was a cup of coffee. The sweets would call out to you from inside their prison like sirens on the rocks, as though the customer was some hapless sailor passing through the dark seas, a sailor who would soon be seeking out the source of the beautiful siren voice.

Just one piece, sang the key lime pie, but Walt ignored the call as he always did. Instead, he replied to T, "I said, where's my burger, T? Did you have to butcher the cow or what?"

T walked from behind the counter and over to Walt's table with a plate that held what could be referred to as the best burger in the area and an order of fries on the side. It looked like one of those billboard advertisements or a picture from a page in a magazine. It was so tantalizing, and it made Walt's mouth water just looking at it.

"Dude, did you just say something?" T asked again.

"Never mind," Walt responded. "Got a fresh bottle of ketchup?" He had a phobia about open bottles of ketchup that sat at the table for days and were refilled over and over. He always asked for a new, unopened bottle and usually used more than half of it on his food. Once he even told someone at work that the only reason he ate French fries was because it made people look at him like he was nuts when he licked the dripping ketchup off his fingers.

"Comin' atcha!"

Walt shoved a handful of fries in his mouth and immediately spit them out on his plate with a muffled "HOT!"

Three

Walt stopped in front of his house and looked up at the peeling sign above the front door. "Antiques and Oddities," it read. The antique store had belonged to Walt's mother. She had been quite a recluse, cooping herself up in the dusty store, never venturing out for weeks on end.

Walt could not remember his mother ever having a single friend. When she died suddenly of an aneurism, he discovered that she had left the store and the building to him, along with what he had thought was a considerable amount of cash, which had only lasted about six months after he paid for her funeral.

She had always said to Walt that he and the store were all she had since his father had left them. He had left her years before, forcing her to singlehandedly run the business and care for their infant son. It was a story that Walt had heard time and time again as he was growing up.

In fact, it was a story that each time was told added another link to the invisible chain that kept Walt tied there. Even though he had a job that paid well enough for him to have his own apartment, he continued to live with the woman who had brought him into this world. Walt dared not dream of the day he could be free of it.

Out of the blue one day, his mother sat down on her chair at the kitchen table. She stared at Walt with a glassy look in her eyes and silently willed him to come closer. She had time to utter the words, "Don't believe what he tells you, there is no way to save your..." then she slumped forward, hitting the table with a thud, and was gone.

Now the store was his, and so was the two-bedroom apartment full of antiques above it.

He tread slowly up the metal steps at the side of the building, and pulled his keys from his pocket to unlock the door. As he positioned his key and reached for the door, he noticed it was cracked open about an eighth of an inch. *What the fuck?*

There were no lights on inside. Instinctively, Walt thought of burglars lurking beyond the door. His mind was racing. Did he lock the door when he left? Had the house been broken into? After his encounter with the young thug earlier this evening, he once again could feel his heart pounding up in his throat as the adrenaline rushed into his bloodstream, his senses on high alert.

He pulled the 9mm from his pocket, crouched low and kicked the door open while simultaneously reaching to turn on the lights. He burst through the door charged into the apartment, nearly knocking over a lamp and.... nothing.

Walt cleared each room just like he'd seen the cops on TV, saying the word "Clear!" out loud, like he had backup or something. Nothing and no one was there. The door to the stairway that led down to the shop was locked as he had kept it since mother had passed. A quick look around and he saw nothing apparently missing.

Obviously, he must have left the door unlocked when he left that morning, but the realization of it was not enough to stop the pounding in his chest. He went to the refrigerator and opened the door, grabbing a beer from the shelf and closing it again. Walt twisted off the top with a "shhhp" and settled into his favorite chair.

The living room of his apartment was still full of the things his mother had collected over the years. It didn't really feel like it belonged to him. In fact, the entire apartment was an assortment of antiques and collectibles. The chairs and tables, the lamps and pictures, all of them antique.

Walt looked at the old photos on the walls. He wasn't sure if he was related to any of the sepia-toned people who stared back at him. The only picture he was sure of was the one of his mother and father taken together on their wedding day.

Mother had told him many times how the wedding day was the happiest day of her life. Most of their hometown had attended back then and that was probably about five years before he was born.

Walt never knew his father. He was gone before Walt was born, and with nothing to hold her, Walt's mother had moved here and opened this store with money she had been saving. At least that was the story he had heard over and over again.

He was on his fourth beer when he finally drifted off to sleep.

Walt rarely had dreams. He had heard about the flying dream and the falling off the cliff dream, but he'd never experienced them. He didn't dream in color when he did dream, always black and white and always the same dream.

Typically, the dream would begin with Walt in the bedroom of this very apartment. He would find himself walking into the living room when the door to the stairway leading to the shop would unlock itself and the knob would turn. The door would slowly swing open without a sound.

Walt would dream walk toward the stairs, which were bathed in an eerie light. Stepping silently through the doorway as if in a trance and then down each step to the door at the bottom, which would open to let him inside.

As the dream continued inside the shop, Walt could see the tables and chairs, lamps and books, all stacked just as they were the day mother died. No dust coating them, no cob webs, everything in its place.

There were dishes, silverware, cases with cheap antique watches and costume jewelry, but he wouldn't even stop to look at those. Lamps, records, and all kinds of junk made up the inventory, and Walt had once wondered why anyone would buy any of it.

Always, in the dreams, he would go over to a table in the back room. Next to the table, boxes were neatly stacked, concealing the shelf beneath it. Walt would always bend over the boxes and slide them over to one side. On the shelf under the table was a small wooden crate. This crate was very well built with thick boards and small, but strong, brass screws.

Every time Walt experienced the dream, he would stoop down and peer at the crate. He would reach his hand out to touch it and, that very moment, a bright blue flash of light would wake him up. Over and over, the same blue light would bring him back to consciousness. No matter how many times he dreamed the dream, he could never touch the box.

This night, Walt sat dreamlessly sleeping in his mother's favorite chair with the half empty beer bottle still in his hand. His mind was a little hazy when he awoke, and looking at the clock, he realized it was just about 11 p.m., his normal bedtime. He got up and headed to the bathroom to brush his teeth.

As he looked at himself in the antique mirror, Walt decided that maybe tomorrow, since it was Saturday, he would go down to the shop after breakfast and see if this box might really exist. He spit the toothpaste out in the sink and lowered his head and rinsed his mouth under the running faucet.

Turning off the bathroom light, Walt trudged to his bed and climbed in. On the night table next to the bed was a book that he was reading on nights when he couldn't sleep, but tonight he didn't need the book. He was tired enough from the stress of the day. When his head hit the pillow, he began to dream the dream.

Four

A call reporting the screams came to the 911 switchboard around 11:30 p.m., and Detective John Hazard was home, just about to close his eyes and sleep when the phone beside his bed rang. He looked at the alarm clock on his nightstand and, groaning, reached over and answered it.

"This better be a damn good-looking woman calling to stop by for some late night fun, or a damn important emergency!"

The voice on the other end didn't hesitate. "Sorry John, we got a winner here. It might be a murder-suicide or maybe a pissed off boyfriend. Either way, looks like the girlfriend put up a fight cuz there's quite a mess and we're really not sure what to make of it. You better come take a look."

"Marcus," John grumbled sarcastically. "So glad you called. I was just settling in for a couple of good nightmares, but it looks like I can have that tonight without even closing my eyes." He sighed. "I'll be there in about twenty if you tell me where *there* is.""2670 Maple Street, and be sure to bring your shoe protectors."

"Not only will I bring my shoe protectors, I'll bring lollipops for the kiddies," replied the detective. Rubbing his eyes to wake himself up, he hung up the phone and rolled out of the covers.

He lifted the pair of pants he had carefully draped across the chair next to his bed not moments before. Slipping them on and fastening his belt, he picked up the black sweater folded there on the seat and pulled it over his head. John rubbed his head as if to comb through his hair, then grabbed his gun and his badge from the nightstand while stepping into his slip-on shoes. His keys seemed to jangle annoyingly loud in the darkness as he grabbed them up and went out to his car.

The streets were quiet this time of night, in fact there was not often much crime happening after midnight in this part of town since the gang control unit was established. Even though there was not much use for real gang control in this little town, it helped to keep the kids off the streets late at night.

Most of the calls that came in these days were for barking dogs and the occasional drunken argument, so a murder would be quite out of the ordinary.

When John arrived on the scene, the other officers had already set up the perimeter tape. Two patrol cars with lights flashing sat in the driveway and one on the street.

The seasoned detective pulled out his magnetic flashing light and stuck it on top of his car just to look official before stepping out into the street.

Three uniformed officers met him as he walked up to the porch, all of them drinking coffee. "Hey Hazard," said one of them. "It's a real mess in there, hope you didn't eat before you came."

"Wentworth, you guys were in there already? Hope you didn't touch anything this time!" John replied.

"No way, after the way you went off on us last time, I thought you were going to pull your piece and add to the body count. We just did a quick search and found the bodies. The mess is all yours, just like we found it."

John slipped on his protective shoe covers, some latex gloves and stepped through the open door. There were two bodies immediately visible in the living room. One was a decapitated torso of a woman lying on the floor, her head lying about four feet from the body. The other was a male with a very large butcher knife thrust up and under his chin into his skull, lying very near the head on the floor.

Wentworth stepped up to the open door and said, "We're thinkin' a murder-suicide. Maybe the boyfriend couldn't handle the crap anymore and went off, took out the babe and did himself."

John replied "Well, you might see it that way except when you consider that stabbing yourself in the head from below the chin is one shitty way to kill yourself, and it would take a lot of force to jam a knife in to the handle like this…"

"How many people do you know who would get a shower, wrap a towel around themselves, then cut off their girlfriend's head."

Wentworth stood as though dumbfounded, looking at the detective as he continued on with his theory.

"No, I think we have a suspect on the loose, and we need to start talking to some neighbors. Tell the guys to get their pencils and books out and start knocking on doors. I want to know if anybody saw or heard anything, especially cars in the driveway or someone running away."

"Who did the call come in from?" John looked at Officer Dix. "Talk to that person first."

John Hazard had been a detective for about six years now. Most of the time he spent investigating home break-ins, auto thefts or the occasional missing person.

These days, it seemed like most missing person calls were about young women who had enough of life in a small town and just packed up and left without telling anyone, including their husband or parents. In those cases, John always hated to question the husbands. Some would just sob and wail. It made it difficult to get any answers or specific reasons why they thought their wives would leave.

The parents on the other hand would get pissed if they were asked questions about possible abuse. No one would ever want to admit that it's possible they could have done something to make their child run from them. The standard questioning always meant an extremely heated exchange of words, mostly with the fathers.

The worst thing about it though was, until that case was closed and the wife, girlfriend, or daughter was found, they were all "Persons of Interest." John understood their frustration.

Tonight, in the case of this gruesome murder, he suspected that the "Person of Interest" might indeed be an ex or current lover or someone who the girl knew very well. And that could mean a male or a female lover these days, nothing was as simple as it used to be. John sure missed the old days.

Either way, there was a near standard procedure for finding out who the perp was, and that would be the procedure he would follow tonight. However, just because these things usually turned out about the same each time, it didn't make the job any easier and John would rather be looking for a burglar this time of night.

Right about then, the CSI van pulled up and Amy Drucker got out carrying her small toolkit for collecting fingerprints and evidence samples.

"Amy, it's a mess in there, prepare yourself," said John. "I think we have a perp on the loose, could be somewhere right here in the area, and we're gonna need you to go over everything really careful this time. Let me know right away if you find any distinct footprints or anything that might help in a search."

"Sure, boss," replied Amy as she surveyed the scene before her. "Need blood samples, fibers, and all that stuff?"

John squinted at her silently with a grim look on his face. After a few seconds she mumbled to herself as she started off toward the door, "Guess that would be a big 'yep' then."

"Hey Amy," John shouted after her, "We got a topless in there, so prepare yourself!" She turned and smiled back at him as though he were making a joke at her expense. She rolled her eyes at the detective, and continued through the door.

One, two, three... John began counting to himself. Amy shot back through the doorway and spewed a stream of vomit over the side of the porch.

"Hey Amy, don't contaminate the crime scene," laughed Officer Wentworth as he patted her on the back. "You wouldn't want to end up a suspect in this one and I'd bet there's some of your DNA mixed in with your dinner up there."

John shook his head as he walked out into the night and got into his car, leaving the door open as he sat down. He picked up the radio receiver, and said, "This is Detective Hazard. I'm here at the 2670 Maple Street scene and we need the coroner's wagon down here, so wake them up and get 'em moving."

Five

Rachel was a fiery-haired beauty, with a remarkable body and raging green eyes. Unlike most redheads, her skin did not freckle and this made her even more stunning to behold. She considered herself to be an independent woman in her late twenties. She asserted that independence on a nightly basis, sleeping with whomever she pleased to fulfill her sometimes-ravenous sexual appetite.

On this particular night, however, she had misjudged the guy who escorted her home and now she was experiencing the consequences of her decision.

Shivering uncontrollably, Rachel's teeth chattered occasionally like one of those wind-up toys. Not only was the night air colder than normal for this time of year, but the blood covering her blouse had chilled and was beginning to get really sticky. She could not remember if she had a coat on when she'd left the house earlier. If so, she had no idea where she had left it.

The ugly black streaks marking the skin below her eyes made it apparent she had been crying. She walked as fast as she could, trying to get home before anyone might ask her questions she did not want to answer.

Arriving home a little out of breath, she went straight to the bathroom and turned on the light. Rachel looked at herself in the mirror.

"Oh my God!" she sobbed, bending over to turn the faucet on in the tub. Letting the hot water run about a minute, finally she climbed in, clothes, shoes and all.

Rachel closed her eyes and let the warmth of the bath ease her shaking body. As the bloody rose-colored water swirled around her, she just curled up to one side in a semi-fetal position and began to sob uncontrollably.

She had never killed anyone before, and she was pretty freaked out. Until tonight, Rachel considered herself to be just another lonely person in a pretty lonely world. She had been looking for love in all the wrong places, and definitely with the wrong person tonight. Now, she was a killer.

She thought back over the events of the evening and, though it seemed like she was just waking up from some kind of crazy nightmare, her bloody clothes gave proof that it was real indeed.

Earlier that night, Rachel had been hanging out down at the Mainline Tavern, just like every other night, having a few drinks, smiling at the guys who glanced her way, and drifting away to sounds from the jukebox when a not-so-bad-looking stranger came over and offered to buy her a drink.

Todd didn't say whether he had a girlfriend and she never asked about those kinds of entanglements. Never. It was a rule she had made for herself a long time ago. She figured if they were interested in her even though they already had someone in their life, well they must not be too happy with what they had. In fact, all she really cared about was a little male company once in a while and a little bit of fun. She wasn't in it to attach any strings. Todd's toothy smile led her to believe he would do just fine for tonight.

After a couple of beers and a few shots, Rachel liked him even better and soon they were having quite a time, laughing and carrying on, her hanging onto his arm and every word he said. Todd wasn't used to that kind of attention, so he was really enjoying himself.

After a couple hours or so of what they used to call 'heavy petting' in a booth over in the corner, Todd whispered that his place was close by and they could have some more intense fun if they went over there for a while. That was cool with Rachel. She was definitely ready for something more intense. They had gotten into his Honda and headed out.

Todd was pretty buzzed since he had not eaten all night, and on the way to his house he drove up on the sidewalk a couple of times. Rachel was buzzed too, so instead of paying attention to his driving skills, she'd just closed her eyes and hummed to herself.

Here in the tub, she realized if she had actually been alert enough to the way he was driving, she might have insisted on getting out of the car and walking home. But she'd been in it to win it, and determined that nothing was going to keep that from happening tonight.

When they'd arrived, Todd let her in through the front door and motioned toward the living room. "Hey baby," he'd said like he'd known her for a long time. "I went out right after I got off work and I'm feeling a bit grimy. Would you mind waiting while I get a quick shower?"

"No problem." She had taken a seat on the oversized sofa.

Rachel recalls hearing the shower water running and the bathroom door close. The sofa was really comfortable, one of those big leather ones with lots of padding. She laid back and kicked her feet up, resting there for a second, until she'd noticed Todd's sound system on the bookshelf.

While most people she knew had moved on to the latest technology, Todd still had something of a CD collection. She thumbed through the plastic boxes, looking for something she might enjoy. It seemed he was into a combination of rock and country, but mostly it was just the classic stuff from the Seventies and Eighties. Not exactly her taste, but it was better than the sound of the dogs barking outside for setting the mood.

Just as Rachel had reached for the power button on the stereo, she could hear keys jangling outside the front door. Someone was inserting the key in the lock and the doorknob was turning.

Rachel had quickly moved into the kitchen before the front door could open and looked for something to defend herself with. It could have been a burglar or, even worse, a home invasion. She could still feel her heart pounding as she thought about the home invasions she had heard about on the news. She didn't want to be the next unlucky victim that didn't stand a chance when the bad guys came through the door. No way. She was not going to be a sitting duck!

Hiding in the shadows, Rachel had frantically looked around. *There must be something here I can use as a weapon!* Panic had begun to set in, and then she'd laid eyes on it.

Lying on the counter next to the sink was a large cutting board and the biggest butcher knife she had ever seen. She quietly picked up the knife and moved back to the doorway hiding the heavy blade behind her back.

"Todd, are you here?" Rachel remembers the woman in the living room calling out.

From her vantage point, she could see the dark-haired beauty with bronzed skin that looked like she held a lifelong membership to a tanning spa.

The woman had seemed fairly harmless as she took off her jacket and set her purse on the sofa. Well-dressed, she appeared to be someone you'd run into at one of those high-end fashion stores in the mall. For a moment, Rachel had dropped her guard and stepped through the doorway out of the kitchen.

"Hi, Todd's in the shower, he should be out in a minute," Rachel remembers trying to sound innocent enough. "I didn't know he was expecting anyone. He didn't mention you were coming by. I'm Rachel, by the way." Rachel, still hiding the knife in her other hand, had reached out to the other woman.

She'd stared back with jaw dropped. Her eyes had grown wide and a tiny vein had appeared just under the surface of the skin on her forehead. After hyperventilating a few moments, she'd screamed at Rachel, "Who the fuck are you?"

Rachel had watched as a spray of spit left the raging woman's lips. *Oh shit...* she'd thought to herself, but then somewhat emboldened by the tone of the woman's question, something inside her had risen up (maybe it was the alcohol). She'd thrown the question right back at her.

"Who the fuck are you?"

"I'm Sara, you whore," as if Rachel should have known, "Todd's fiancée? That son of a bitch didn't tell you he was engaged?"

Rachel could have sworn she'd seen flames coming from Sara's mouth just then.

Sara had been suspicious of Todd for weeks, believing that he had been sleeping with another woman. She had accused him several times of it and, even though he denied it repeatedly, she had never been able to catch him.

Jealous obsession led her to do some crazy things she had never done before. She found herself checking his phone for messages, following him on her days off when he did not spend them with her, and asking his friends about what he may have said to them about her.

Finally it seemed she had caught him in the act. He *was* cheating on her with this redheaded slut, and there was only one thing she could think of to do about it.

Without warning, Sara had attacked. A coffee table and sofa were all that stood between her and the object of her rage. In a quick 1-, 2-, 3-step movement, Sara had jumped onto the coffee table and propelled herself over the sofa at Rachel. It was like watching a basketball star going in for the layup, but this was no game for Sara.

Instinctively, her arms had thrust out with a forceful self-protective motion. Acting purely on reflex, Rachel had been stunned when the blade of the large knife she held firmly in her hand met with her assailant's neck in one bone-grinding movement.

The weight of Sara's body and the force of her leap provided enough force against the blade. Rachel's stiffened arms, thrust out in fear, created the perfect conditions necessary to sever Sara's head completely from her body. It must have been a very, very sharp knife.

In a spray of blood, and with a muffled "ugh," Sara's headless body had fallen to the floor with a thud. As her head rolled to a stop on the kitchen rug, the expression of surprise had appeared in her widened eyes for only a moment before her life had faded away.

Rachel recoiled as she thought of it again, and her body shook violently again from the shock. She could recall that her arms were jerking reflexively as she'd picked up the knife and stared at it in disbelief. Her fist had clenched around the knife as a dark red pool of Sara's blood had spread across the floor as it had spewed, slower then from her twitching torso.

Rachel's mouth had formed a silent scream. Tears streamed from her eyes at the realization of what she had done. Her hopes and dreams for the future passed before her eyes as she had imagined what would happen next.

Prison.

Death sentence?

It's over.

Suddenly she found her voice and the sound of her pitiful, shrieking wail echoed through the house. She had tried to sit down but she couldn't. She could only stand there twitching and grasping the knife in a white knuckled grip. With all of the commotion and ensuing shock, she had not heard the shower turn off.

"What the hell is going on out there?" Todd had yelled out.

There was no answer, just the sound of Rachel sobbing.

He must have grabbed a towel from the rack and stepped out of the shower leaving a path of wet footprints as he dripped his way to the door. As he stepped into the room, it was then he must have caught sight of the blood on the floor. Looking around he probably saw the red spray on the walls and sofa as he'd moved closer. Todd had stopped there stunned by what he found, a woman's headless body on the floor.

"What the fuck did you do, who is this?!?" he'd screamed. Then he realized it was Sara's head lying there on his kitchen rug.

"Oh shit! Sara!" he shrieked as he'd bent over and touched her bloodied shoulder.

Rachel stood herself up and was backing away when Todd's attention turned to her. For a moment, he'd glared at her, his nostrils flared like a wild dog and then... snarling like some enraged animal, he'd charged her.

Again she'd held up her hands to defend herself and as she did, Todd had spotted the bloody knife she was still holding and reached for it.

He'd moved too quickly, his footing probably compromised by his wet bare feet. There was no way Todd could have steadied his balance when his foot hit the blood soaked area where Sara had been decapitated. Rachel could still see him trying to catch himself as his feet ran faster than he could go, like some cartoon character on Saturday morning TV, but he'd stumbled forward toward Rachel.

Todd was somewhat of an athlete and Rachel could tell that he'd prided himself on his quick reflexes. He'd told her some stories earlier at the bar. Now he nimbly snatched the knife from Rachel's hand even as he was falling, but he couldn't control his momentum.

As he'd stiffened his arms to break his fall, the knife he'd grabbed was still pointing toward him in an awkward vertical position. Todd was just about to hit the floor when the realization of what was about to happen must have struck him.

"Oh shit!" The last words he would ever say escaped his lips as he'd crashed to the floor.

The impact of his fall had caused the knife to hold firm, with point up and handle down. Todd's head arced toward the tip of the blade, and he'd landed chin first, driving the knife firmly through his lower jaw and into his skull, pinning his mouth and jaw shut.

Rachel's shock was compounded as she remembered how Todd's body lay twitching on the floor, his hands helplessly seeking to pull the handle of the knife. Suddenly, Todd's writhing motion had stopped and timed seemed to stop as the house had fallen silent. Todd's lifeless eyes had fixed on her as if pleading for her help.

There was nothing she could have done.

Rachel recalled how she had stared at the horrific carnage her promised night of 'intense fun' had caused. She knew she was the reason two people had died there tonight, and in such a nightmarish scene she could not have believed just a couple of hours ago.

She'd panicked. She'd taken one step, and then carefully stepped over Todd's body. Putting one seemingly leaden foot in front of the other, Rachel had forced her legs to keep on going. At last, she'd gone through the open door and down the steps to the sidewalk.

"I just want to go home now, Mommy." Childlike, she had whimpered to herself.

Rachel rolled over in the tub and hugged herself in a self-protective pose, squeezing her eyes closed more tightly to shut out the memories.

Six

Saturday morning and it was cool and rainy in Walt's world. The weather could not affect his plan for the day though. Walt was looking forward to venturing into his mother's antique shop below. It was around 8 a.m., so coffee was the prerequisite of any activity of the day.

As Walt measured three scoops of coffee, he went over his dream from the night before. It always seemed so real. Each time he entered the antique shop in the dream, he always seemed so sure that he would find something when he looked below the table in the back room. He was planning to look for the crate this morning. It seemed absurd to feel so sure that he would find it.

He filled the coffee pot from the faucet to the line indicating four cups, poured it into the coffeemaker, and pressed the button to begin the brew. Walt lumbered across the room and switched on the television. At this time of the morning, the local news was still on and the weather girl was talking about the forecast of rain followed by sunshine later that afternoon.

Clearly, it was raining this morning, but whether it would actually be followed by sunshine was the real question. The way he saw the weather, if you want to know what the weather is, look outside. If you want to know what it will be like tomorrow, take a guess. That is all the weather forecasters can do.

Walt stood for a moment, watching the coffee drip into the pot, then went into the bedroom and put on some jeans and a sweatshirt, white socks, and some old work shoes.

He walked to the bathroom mirror and ran a comb through his thinning hair. "Lay down," he commanded and held the comb under some running water to plaster his unruly hair in place.

The smell of freshly brewed coffee drew him to the kitchen.

There was a reporter on the TV now talking about a double homicide that occurred during the night. Apparently, the cops had originally theorized that the gruesome deaths of the man and woman were a murder-suicide, but some detective – Walt didn't catch his name – had determined that a third person had been involved and was now being sought for questioning.

Right about then the coffeepot made a high pitched beeping sound, indicating the end of the brew cycle and letting Walt know that his first cup of the morning was ready to pour. He walked over to the cupboard and pulled out a box of Fruity Flakes, a coffee mug, and a cereal bowl.

First things first, he filled the mug with hot steaming coffee. Opening the refrigerator, he got out the milk. He poured some into his coffee but not on the Fruity Flakes. He preferred to eat them dry just like when he was a kid. It made it seem like more of a meal than just a sloppy bowl of soggy flakes.

Sipping his coffee, Walt sat down at the table. He was thinking about his dream again, and wondered again whether the crate he was looking for actually existed. It would be easy to imagine such a thing, but then it could easily turn out to be just a dream.

He had often considered the dusty shelves in his mother's store and all of the old things they contained. Sometimes he imagined that ghosts of all the people who previously owned those objects might inhabit the store, or even the objects themselves. It made him smile as he imagined rubbing his antique cereal bowl and having a genie appear to grant his wishes.

The Fruity Flakes tasted better than usual this morning for some reason, and he washed each bite down with a swallow of coffee. When Walt had finished the last bite, he carried his bowl over to the sink and rinsed it with hot water, like always, and put it in the dish drainer. He had learned from mother that it is easier to clean as you go, rather than letting things like dirty dishes pile up

A refill of coffee to go, and he started looking for the keys to the door that led to the antique shop. He thought he remembered putting them in the junk drawer along with everything else that didn't have an urgent purpose. As he pulled the drawer open, papers caught on the bottom of the counter and popped out, fluttering to the floor.

"Fucking coupons, don't know why I even bother with them," he said to himself. "Guess that's an old mom habit."

He recalled how his mother had saved and collected everything. *Never know when it might come in handy…* she'd say. By the time she died, the apartment was nearly stacked floor to ceiling with old newspapers and magazines. From what he could tell, none of them ever 'came in handy.'

After the funeral, Walt had hired a company to put a dumpster below the landing on the stairs. It took him nearly a week to carry out all the garbage that was "saved" in the apartment and toss it into the dumpster. He had never really known up to that point what the apartment actually looked like. It was an obsession his mother had before he was born.

Once he'd asked her why she subscribed to so many different publications. Her response had been quite vague, something like, "I need to watch what's happening in other parts of the world, see if there is anything strange or unexplained." When he asked her to elaborate, she had simply said, "Oh baby, it is nothing to worry your head about, just eat your Fruity Flakes so you can grow up to be big and strong." Then she smiled that smile that meant it was all the explanation he was going to get, and he never asked that question of her again.

Clearing away the top clutter of the junk drawer, Walt surveyed the contents below. Pens, pencils, chip clips, screws, pliers, note pads, calculator, scotch tape, masking tape, tape measures, a Democratic Party membership card, and at the bottom of it all, in the very back, a ring of old brass keys. He put them in his pocket and, with the whole length of his arm, scraped everything back into the drawer.

Walking over to the television, Walt switched it off and turned toward the door that led down the stairs to the shop. With the key ready in his hand now, he reached the door, slid the key easily into the lock and turned it. There was a loud click as the door unlocked. With the door opened only enough for his arm to fit through, he flipped the light switch on the wall next to the door, and suddenly realized why he hadn't done this before now.

Immediately he was filled with dread. He had forgotten the stacks of newspapers and magazines that had been stored temporarily on the stairs. Before he could go down into the shop using this stairwell, he would have to clean it up.

He stood at the top of the stairs and stared at the mess for a moment. A few of the stacks had fallen over and, like dominoes, had taken other stacks with them as they tumbled to the landing below.

Now he had to choose: clean up the mess, or go outside and around to the front door.

Front door it should be, but still he felt compelled to clean up the mess and before the end of the day. Why did he have to feel this way just now when all he really wanted to do is to follow through on his vision?

He walked over and picked up the phone. He even remembered the phone number, 1-800-JUNKPUNK. Sure, the last letter did not really count, but it was known throughout the state as one of the most memorable phone numbers for a business - ever. Now Walt understood why they said that. He dialed.

Ring.

Ring.

Then a message, "Thanks for calling the Junk Punk. If you need to order a cleanup bin press one, if you need to request a pickup, press two, for all other calls press three."

Walt pressed one and waited.

"All of our representatives are currently helping others to clean up their act, please remain on the line and we'll gladly help you to un-clutter your life too."

Walt sat down in his Mom's favorite old chair and listened to the music on hold, a hardcore metal-techno-hip hop remix of old Elvis Presley songs. After a few minutes, someone came on the line.

"Hello, thanks for calling the Junk Punk, got some shit you wanna throw away?" asked a female voice that sounded like she'd been gargling glass.

"Uh, yeah," stammered Walt. "I called about a year ago and had a dumpster delivered, um, one of those really big ones, but I think I just need a smaller one this time. Can you deliver one today?"

"Oh, can you say 'Hell, Yes we can'?" Her voice grated on Walt's nerves.

"What was the name or phone number on the account?" Walt gave her his number.

"Hey is this Walter? Walter Turner?" she asked. "I got you man. I think we can have a can there in about an hour. You cool with that?" she said with machine-gun-like bursts.

"Yeah," replied Walt. *Zeesh, what a freakin' harpy!*

"Ok then, same piece of plastic?"

"Huh?"

"Ah, credit card, dude…" she croaked.

"Oh. Yeah, same piece," said Walt.

"It's rollin', man… as… we… speak…" She hung up the phone without a thank-you or a good-bye.

Walt held the phone out from his ear with a puzzled look, studying it for a minute before turning it off and setting it back on the charger.

The Junk Punk was proud to brag that they had a reputation like an old whore. They had rightfully earned it for being fast, cheap, and easy to work with. They never asked too many questions. They had the best service in the business, so most people just put up with their crap. Walt was just happy they could deliver today, in an hour no less.

Thirty minutes later, the roar of a truck in the alley and the warning beep, beep, beep as it backed up alerted him that the can had arrived. Walt went out to the landing and yelled at the driver. "Hey, just drop it right here below the landing and open the lid before you leave, I want to throw stuff in it from here."

"Yeah? OK, man," responded the driver.

Walt went back in the house and tried to mentally prepare for a long morning of hauling paper. He hated this shit. Why had his mother been so obsessed with saving every scrap of paper?

Seven

It was about two in the afternoon when John finally woke up. He had been up until nearly four in the morning, locking up the crime scene and finishing his paperwork.

The sun was streaming through the blinds, and dust particles danced in the light as he rolled out of bed. He put some pants on and sat on the edge of the bed scratching his head. He had a lot of work to do today. Neighbors to interview, evidence to review, and oh, there was his favorite, the trip to the coroner's office.

As he pulled his half buttoned shirt over his head, he decided he would do the coroner's office first, then go by the office to see what other evidence had been gathered by the CS team. He knew he'd have to review any potential witness statements, if there *were* any, and though it always helped to put the pieces of the puzzle together, he never did enjoy interviewing a lot of witnesses.

He walked into the bathroom and looked at himself in the mirror.

"*You* look like shit," he pointed at the mirror before greasing his toothbrush with some minty paste and shoving into his mouth. Once around, inside and out of the pearly whites, and he spit into the sink, twisting his head down to the faucet to rinse.

Still looking at himself in the mirror, he buttoned his shirt and tucked it in, fastened his belt, ran his hands over his short cropped hair and went to the nightstand for his gun, badge and cell phone. John grabbed his jacket from the back of his chair and he was out the door.

He was almost to his car when he turned around, went back into the house and headed straight to the bathroom. Grabbing the can of spray deodorant off the back of the toilet, one shot to each armpit, and he was on his way again.

He had only gone about a block when his phone rang and he answered. "It's John," he answered, "tell me something good."

"Hey, John," said the voice on the other end. "Your doctor called and said not to worry, the head up your ass is yours and other than that you'll survive."

"Frank," replied John flexing his mouth to one side in a half grimace. "Thanks for the update, got anything else for me?"

"Nothing much, Hazard," said Frank, "except I've got this fine figure of a woman down here who seems to have lost her head over her boyfriend. You on your way or do I need to send a car to pick you up at the Mainline?"

"Yeah, right," said John. "I'll be there in ten. Save a place in the cooler for me."

Around 2:30, John rolled into the coroner's office parking lot. On the weekends, there were not many cars around. Seemed like, in this town, there wasn't a lot of death on weekends for some reason. Most people had the decency to wait until at least Monday morning to kick it if they had a mind to do such a thing.

When John walked into the examination room, Frank was weighing some kidneys.

"Hey, Frankie, howzabout a serving of those with some mashed potatoes and gravy?" John always tried to make light of the situation while there. As a rookie, he had learned that it helped him push away any squeamishness on his part.

"Yeah, go ahead and make a joke. When it's your turn on the table, I'll leave you out in the hall naked and uncovered for the day with a permanent marker so everyone can autograph you when they pass by!"

"Okay, point taken," John said. "Any results from last night yet?"

Frank walked over to the wall of cooler doors at the other end of the room, grabbed a handle and pulled out the large tray. On it was Todd's body covered by a sheet. Frank pulled back the sheet and said, "This one, Todd, I believe, was an accidental death. When I removed the knife he was wearing below his chin, there were fibers from the towel he had wrapped around him on his hand and all over the handle. This tells me that *he* was the one holding the knife when it went in. If it was murder in this case, I would be able to tell just from the angle it went through below the chin. No, I think he fell on the blade."

He turned and opened the door on his other side and pulled out the tray. "Now, Marie Antoinette here is kind of a puzzler… If I was a betting man, I'd say that there was so much force when her neck was severed, she would have to be airborne when it happened. Not to mention the marks on the shoulder and head most likely indicating trauma as she hit the floor after the deed was done."

"I have to admit, in all of my years in this job, I have never seen the likes of these two coming from the same crime scene," added Frankie. "This is some weird shit for this town, my friend. Weird shit. But it *does* make the job more interesting, I must admit."

"So, are you saying that the girl was flying when she lost her head?" John said.

"Well, it kinda seems that way. At least to me anyway… but, more accurately, airborne as if she was lunging at her killer." Frank gestured as though he were about to dive at Hazard.

"You see," he went on, "normally to decapitate somebody ya gotta saw at it a little but, in this case, the cut was powerful and clean, right through the cartilage between the vertebrae."

"So you think it is a murder-suicide then? Is that what you're saying?" John demanded.

"Well, not exactly, but I *will* say I've never seen anything like it before," Frank answered. "I suggest you look carefully at the crime scene photos before you call it."

John shook his head in response. He took one more look at Todd's body and said, "Was there any sign of sexual activity before this happened?"

"I didn't find anything like that. Everything looked squeaky clean, if you catch my drift…" Frank smiled. "Why, you thinking about getting some 'head' now, Hazard?" He finished the sentence in a roar of laughter.

John snorted, "Damn, I knew you coroners were sick, but I had no idea the depths of depravity that exists in your world."

Frank's laughter ended in a coughing fit, and he choked out, "Takes one to know one buddy!" and slapped the detective on the back.

Eight

"Finally, the last load", Walt muttered to himself as he picked up the final stack of magazines. He carried them up the steps, across the living room, out the door and dropped them in the dumpster which by now was filled to about eight inches from the top.

He sat down on the top step for a minute to take a break and wiped the sweat from his forehead on his shirtsleeve.

Heading back into the house, Walt picked up the phone to call for a pick up. Since it was only about three o'clock, he figured he might be able to get the dumpster removed before the end of the day. He dialed and this time a real person answered directly.

A husky male voice gave the standard greeting. "Hello, thanks for calling the Junk Punk, got some shit to throw away?" Before Walt could answer, he heard the hold music and then... nothing.

"Hello?"

"Oh, sorry dude, lost it for a second there, can I help you?"

"Uh, yeah, well I have a dumpster that needs to be picked up," said Walt. "It was delivered earlier today, and now it's filled and ready to go. Can you get it before the end of the day?"

"Wait a sec," the man answered and put him on hold. There was no music this time and after about 20 seconds he came back on the line. "Yeah dude, we can get it in about an hour, you cool wit dat?""

"Yeah."

"What's your name or number? Who should I say wants their dumpster picked up?"

Walt gave his number.

"Ok, my people will be right over, have a good one!"

Click.

Once again, Walt held the phone out and looked at it. Shaking his head, he set it back in the charger. Then he walked over to the refrigerator and opened the door, looked in and grabbed a can of beer. He popped the top and sat down at the table.

He took a deep breath and allowed himself to relax for a moment. Walt enjoyed the moment of darkness that came from closing his eyes, and listened to his breath moving in and out of his body. It was while in this deeply relaxed mode that an image gradually formed in his mind. A table. A shelf below it. A wooden crate on the shelf.

This was the very same vision that often came to him even when he was awake, but this time the vision came with his name written in red on the top of the box. It appeared to be written with a red grease pencil. Mother always used a red grease pencil. She was old-fashioned that way.

Walt sat up straight and opened his eyes. His gaze went to the open door to the stairwell. He took another long swig of his beer.

He thought about going down into the shop right now, but he thought better of it when he remembered the last time the dumpster was picked up. They needed his signature on the invoice. He might miss the driver if he was down in the shop so he resigned himself to waiting.

"I might need a flashlight," he said out loud. "It's probably dark down there." He stood up and walked to his bedroom. He went to the closet and reached up to pull the string for the light switch. A quick snap of his wrist and Walt was left holding the string as the bulb flashed with a pop, then burned out.

"Fuck! Why does everything have to be such a pain in the ass!"

Now he trudged back to the kitchen to find a new light bulb. He opened the cupboard above the refrigerator and found only one bulb left in the box. It was one of those twisty fluorescent bulbs that he had tried to use in the lamp in the living room, but removed it because he decided he didn't like the artificial light.

"Mental note to self," he said. "Buy real light bulbs before you can't find them anymore."

He picked up a pen from the counter and wrote on the magnetic pad hanging on the refrigerator door. At the bottom of the perennial list, he scratched out, "Real light bulbs."

As he walked back into the bedroom, he heard the beep, beep, beep of a truck backing up.

"Damn!"

Walt set the bulb down on the dresser and headed to the door, looking out at the alley. The truck driver was hooking up the dumpster. He looked up and made eye contact. "Hey cousin, want to scratch your name on this invoice for me?" he said, waving the paper over his head.

Walt stepped out of the doorway, tread down the steps, and snatched up the invoice along with the pen that was sticking out of the driver's shirt pocket. He hurriedly signed the paper and stuck the pen in his mouth as he folded the invoice and shoved it into the guy's pocket. Taking the pen out of his mouth, Walt put on a fake smile, then turned and began to walk away without saying a word.

The driver stood staring for a moment. "Hey, dude! You forgot my pen!"

Walt turned on his heel and shoved the pen in the driver's pocket, gave it a condescending little pat, and turned away once more.

The driver forced out a cheery voice, "Have a great fuckin' day, dude!" He walked around the dumpster, clicking the locks in place, then got in his truck and drove away.

Later, when the truck turned onto the freeway, a magazine flew out of the dumpster, landed along side the road and opened to a page with large bold letters on the headline, "Freeze Dried Body of Missing Man Discovered!" The words were circled with red grease pencil.

In the meantime, Walt went back to his room and changed out the light bulb. He was rooting around in the closet. He uncovered the flashlight when he pushed aside the pile of laundry and lifted a soiled pair of boxer shorts sitting in the corner. He picked up the small silver light and pushed the switch with his thumb. It worked!

He turned it off to save the battery and shoved it into his pants pocket. Pulling the cord to turn off the overhead light, Walt walked out of the closet swinging the door shut behind him. He was thinking about the vision he'd had earlier and hesitated mid-step.

What if he found the box from his vision? How could he know it was there when he had never actually seen it? If it was real, did it have some kind of ability to let him know it was there? There was really only one way to find out. He headed again for the stairway.

He had left the light on after the last load and, as Walt took each step, he had the sensation that somehow the stairway was twisting before him. By the time he reached the bottom of the stairs, he was breathing heavily as though he'd been going up a long stairway, not down. He guessed he was just tired from carrying all of those newspapers and magazines.

Walt reached for the doorknob. The door to the shop was locked. He fished in his pocket for the keys, took them out and tried the first one. It was not the right one.

The key ring had five keys, two silver, two brass, and one key that was entirely black. He had never seen a black key before, so he tried the black one next. As he turned it in the lock it made a strange *whoosh* as if there was some sort of air pressure inside the lock.

He turned the knob and opened the door. Next to the doorframe was a light switch just where you'd expect it to be. Walt flipped it on and lit up the shop for the first time since Mother had died.

He'd nearly forgotten what the shop looked like. The last time he had been down here was about a year ago, and then it was only to make sure the heaters were unplugged and the back door was locked securely.

Walt hadn't been interested to look through anything down here, or even to sell it. He'd figured that someday he might have an auction, or maybe sell all this junk on a website somewhere.

After Mother died, everything about it seemed too difficult to accomplish, and Walt wanted no part of it. A few people had offered to buy the shop from him, but somehow he didn't want to sell it to a stranger. Mother had put so much of her life into it. In fact, when it came to the antique shop, Walt had a lot of mixed feelings. For the most part, confusion, some feelings of uncertainty, at least until now.

For a few moments, he stood there and looked around. It seemed the antique shop had never looked the way it did today. It was as though he was seeing it for the first time.

He knew he'd played in here when he was a child. Mother often told him how he would offer to help the customers and pretend to be the shopkeeper. Mother told him a lot about his childhood. For some reason, he could not seem to remember it for himself. Could be something traumatic had happened to make his subconscious block it out, but like everything else about his early years, if there had been some tragedy, he had no idea what it might have been.

Maybe the shop seemed different today simply because his mother was not here. In life, she had been a powerful force of a woman. For all of her strange traits, and though she had become more and more of a recluse, she was loved by many people.

Walt could remember being at the shop while friend after friend of his mother's would drop by to visit. They'd spend hours talking and laughing and gossiping about the neighborhood. When the visit was over, they'd always make a small purchase before they left.

On the counter where the cash register sat, there was a beautiful cabinet made of mahogany and leaded glass. That was where the *real* treasures were placed until they found a new location in some customer's home. Mother had once commented that the cabinet was hundreds of years old and had a history that no one really knew, although she seemed to be an expert. When Walt was younger, he imagined that it was something magical.

When the afternoon sunlight would come in through the front window, the beveled edges of the glass cabinet would throw tiny rainbows all about the room and as the sun dipped even lower, the rainbows would seem to swirl around on the walls.

Each week, new items were hand selected from the shop inventory. Items that had seemed damaged, rusted, worn out, or just plain broken. To Walt, it had seemed bizarre, even magical, that when these inferior items went from bookcase shelves to the glass cabinet, they would suddenly become as new sparkling treasures.

Everyone who looked upon these special treasures seemed compelled to buy, no matter what the price. There were times, it seemed to Walt, that people had purchased items that really were of no value at all for a very high price. Maybe all it took was to be labeled "antique" by his mother.

He was just a boy... or was he fully grown then? There was no way for him to separate the memories, but he was sure that there was something strange about the way people acted when they looked into that cabinet.

For instance, one day a woman came by and bought a plain white plate. That plate had been sitting on a bookshelf for months before it went into the glass cabinet, but when this woman saw it she let out a squeal of delight. "It's the plate, it's the plate!" she raved. But it was just a plain white plate that couldn't have been more than five years old.

When the woman had asked Mother, "How much for that precious plate?" She had calmly replied, "Oh, that one, well I didn't really want to sell that one. I really only had it in the cabinet to admire it and allow folks to see it's fine detail and wonderful finish. BUT, if I did want to sell it, what would a fine collector like you, an individual with such obvious taste, offer for such a treasure? Keep in mind that

I'd really rather not sell it now so do not embarrass yourself in front of my dear son by offering less than it is obviously worth."

The woman offered seven hundred dollars! Of course, by the time mother was through with her, that *treasure* of a five year old, plain white plate made in China, fetched over fifteen hundred.

Walt had seen his mother take a doll off of the shelf, take it out of the box in which it was purchased less than a year earlier, wipe it down with her 'lucky' cleaning cloth and place it in the glass cabinet.

It seemed like the next person through the door would look into the cabinet and squeal, "The doll! Oh my God, how much for the doll? My daughter would love to start a doll collection, and what a good way to begin!"

Mother would never, ever put a price on things in the cabinet. If there were a price on the item before she put it there, she would carefully remove it first.

This was the priceless principle: *Things without a price became priceless*. It was an amazing thing to watch how again and again the 'treasures' sold for such large sums of money. It was how his mother paid off the mortgage on the building, cared for Walt and put away a good bit of cash after his father had left.

It was as though his mother was somehow able to blind people to the real value of these so-called antiques. They readily believed that the things were worth whatever she wanted them to be worth.

If Walt didn't know better, he'd believe that maybe she was some kind of real magician, but Walt didn't believe in real magic, only the tricks of showmen who called themselves magicians. Without a doubt, no matter how elaborate the trick might be, all of the magic ever performed was just a well-rehearsed trick created in the fertile imagination of the professional magician.

Nonetheless, there was Walt, standing near the heart of his mother's shop, her 'living glory', as she called it. The collection was the same as it had been on the day she had passed away.

Old tables and furniture, many of the pieces layered with multiple coats of paint, dishes, cast iron pans, dolls, old phonograph records, trinkets, soda bottles, buttons, pins, costume jewelry and things normally reserved for the flea markets. A lot of it obtained when people threw it away, and Walt had spent many hours walking with Mother through the neighborhoods on trash day, picking through the piles of leftover garage sale items.

Without Mother it was just lifeless, cold, and silent junk. All of the life had left the shop when her spirit left this world. Walt thought this might be why he preferred not to come down here.

He turned toward the back of the shop then, where items were piled almost to the ceiling on a variety of tables, desks, and bookcases. There was a cleared out pathway to the backdoor, however. The Fire Marshall had been to the shop and had issued Mother a written warning about six months before she died. He said that there had to be at least a four-foot wide, clear walkway through the store or they would issue a fine for the fire hazard.

Walt remembered even that visit was kind of strange. On the way out of the store, the Fire Marshall had stopped to look into the cabinet. Ten minutes later, he'd left with a big shit-eatin' grin, carrying his 'incredible', new, three hundred dollar shot glass that had a picture of a dolphin on it and the words Miami Beach Florida printed in cheerful green letters.

What a chump!

As Walt walked to the back of the store, he stopped and closed his eyes, trying to remember the dream and visions he'd had about the crate he came down to find. To his right, about three feet in front of him, he saw two piles of books stacked on the floor.

Walt stepped forward for a closer look. Squinting now, he could barely see the corner of a wooden crate showing from behind those books. Could it really be the wooden crate he had seen in his visions?

He could feel his heart beating faster as bent to move the books out of the way. When he slid the second stack over, he could clearly see the crate beneath the old table. He pulled it out from under the table with a true sense of wonder.

It was made of wood that appeared old and weathered, though beautifully finished. This was not some common crate made of pine, but some sort of hardwood, perhaps some variety of oak.

The crate was about twenty-four inches square. More of a cube, it was perfectly shaped, no rough edges or errors in the cut of the wood, more like a case made to hold something in particular.

Something of great value, Walt was guessing.

Walt looked over the surface of the crate again, turning it carefully, half expecting to find a lid with hinges or some way to open it, but there was none. There were screws around the perimeter of the entire crate spaced at one-inch intervals. It appeared that there were maybe a hundred or more small silver screws holding it together.

Why so many screws? He wondered to himself.

Could it be to just to make it more difficult for anyone wanting to open it? Maybe to keep whatever was stored inside from getting out? *Surely whatever was in a crate this small couldn't be all that dangerous.*

Whatever the reason, Walt had decided before he even came down the stairs that, if the crate turned out to be real, he was going to open it and see what was inside it. Nothing was going to stop him, not after all of the bullshit he had gone through!

He picked it up now. He was a little surprised that it wasn't very heavy for something that looked like it was constructed from heavy materials. He turned to head out of the shop and back upstairs. As he walked over to the stairway, the palms of his hands seemed to warm where they were touching the wood. A tingling sensation like a tiny electric shock passed through his fingers.

He shrugged off any feelings of distress, thinking it was just the excitement of discovering his dream had been real. Or maybe it was the strange wood reflecting the heat from his hands. *Who the hell knows what could cause the tingling?*

When Walt had reached the third step up, he missed his footing and tripped. The box tumbled from his arms and bounced down the stairs.

Shit, I hope whatever's in there is packed good and tight! He thought how messed up it would be to finally open the strange crate and find whatever inside broken because of his stupid clumsiness. He carefully picked it up and went back to climbing the stairs.

Walt felt a rush of excitement as he neared the top. *Just a few more steps and we're there.* He said to the crate he was holding. Entering the apartment, he carried the crate directly to the dining table and set it down with ceremony as if it were a sacred object.

He switched on the light that hung over the table and sat down to inspect the strange little crate more closely. Walt turned the crate over and saw his name written on it there.

In red grease pencil… just as in his vision.

It creeped him out, and for a few moments, he just sat there and stared at his name. Without a doubt, it was written in Mother's handwriting.

Walt stood up, scraping his chair as he pushed himself away from the table. He went over to the cupboard beneath the sink and began to fish around in the toolbox there for a small screwdriver. He found just what he needed and returned to the table.

He decided that where his name was written was probably the topside of the crate. Walt began the process of removing each tiny screw and, as he did, he counted them. He set each one carefully into the pile as he went. One, two, three… fifteen, sixteen… nineteen, twenty… eighty screws in all.

He carefully removed the top and set it on the table next to the screws. As he stood up to look inside, suddenly Walt felt dizzy. *Steady, boy… this too shall pass…* but he was suddenly so overcome he sank to his knees on the floor. It wasn't just dizziness, the entire room was spinning out of control and even as he closed his eyes to try to stop the sensation, he could see the blackness of shadows spinning around him.

Is this a dream?

In the silence of the room, he could swear he heard voices. He thought he could make out many voices, maybe as many as fifty or more, all talking or screaming or moaning at the same instant. It was a distant sound that seemed to come closer and then move away. There were many different languages, most that Walt could not recognize let alone understand, and they seemed to swirl around him like the blackness of the shadows. Finally, everything went black.

Nine

He lay there on the floor for about a half hour completely unaware until suddenly he was jolted awake by a voice that screamed "Walt!"

He sat up on the floor, and waited for the dizziness to pass. He realized that he did not feel dizzy anymore. As a matter of fact, he felt as though he'd just awakened from a perfect night of sleep. Actually, he had never in his entire life felt so invigorated.

Walt hopped to his feet and bent over the table to peer into the crate. All he could see was wood shavings. They appeared to be from the same type of wood that the crate was made from. He went back to the sink and got a plastic bag from the grocery store out from under it and returned to the table.

Slowly, Walt reached into the crate and scooped out a handful of the wood shavings. At the third handful, his hand struck something solid. He carefully brushed away the shavings and saw four points sticking up from inside them.

Four golden points.

As he went on removing the shavings, handful-by-handful, Walt finally cleared the way to see what was inside. There was some kind of a box, made of pottery. The top of the box looked like a crown and he could make out what looked like facial features on one side of the box.

Carefully, with both hands, Walt lifted the box from the crate and set it on the table.

It was an incredible piece of pottery. The face on the front of the box was so perfectly carved it appeared to be real. Its eyes were closed, or opened? It was hard to tell because there were no pupils. They had no real definition, and it appeared as though the person who had been modeled in the clay may have been sightless.

The face had a moustache and a short scraggly beard. The nose and chin were classic European: narrow-nosed, medium thin lips. The lid of the box was sort of a squared crown with four short spires and a domed top that was similar to a small pyramid.

Parts of the crown was overlaid with gold and silver leaf, and even in the dull light of the table lamp, it shimmered. *It looks like it's made of some kind of pottery,* Walt thought, *but the face... it kind of looks alive!*

He was a little bit curious and, at the same time, cautious about what this might mean. The crate had his name on it. He'd had a vision or something he couldn't explain. Somehow he'd known that there was a box in the crate, the visions had been that clear.

Now here it was, sitting on the table in his kitchen.

He decided, against all instincts, to remove the crown that appeared to be the lid of the box. He pulled up on the points that made up the crown.

The lid, if it were a lid in fact, would not come off.

So he tilted the box a bit to get a better look at the side of it. Walt couldn't see any seams, or cracks. It appeared to be a solid piece of pottery, but it wasn't heavy enough to be solid clay. It had to be hollow. Maybe it was glued on?

"You can only remove the crown if you are truly worthy to witness my power. You must feel it. Do you feel it, Walt?"

Walt let go of the box and it rocked back to the tabletop with a thud.

"Who's there?!" he yelled while looking around the room. "I gotta fucking gun and I'm not afraid to use it!"

Walt stood up and reached for his coat hanging on one of the chairs. His hands were shaking as he pulled his 9mm from one of the pockets. He turned looking around the open area of the apartment. Almost machine-like, he went through the apartment, clearing it room by room just as he'd done when he'd arrived home the day before to verify that no one was in the apartment.

Finally Walt was satisfied. Not a soul was to be found. He walked to the door and made sure it was locked. He even checked the door to the stairway going down to the shop, and it too was locked.

He was sure that the apartment was secure so he pocketed his gun and walked back over to the table. He sat back down in front of the box and looked into its cold black eyes. They held a blank expression as if, at some moment in a time gone by, a thought was locked within them. They were the eyes of the dead.

"You must be a great warrior." The voice took on a flattering tone. *"You wield your weapon with great confidence and apparent skill. You have experienced victory in past battles."*

Walt jumped back from the chair and whipped the pistol out of his pocket. He whirled around looking in all directions.

"Wh-who are you? Where are you hiding?" He was stuttering and started to shake again. He stood with his back to the box.

"Why do you ask this? I do not hide. I am right behind you as you left me," said the voice. *"Here, on this fine wooden table. You look directly at me, then you turn to seek out ghosts."*

Walt turned around slowly. He was incredulous. The only thing he could see was the box on the table. *I must be crazy*, he thought. *This box could not be talking to me.*

"Indeed, you can hear my voice, Walt. As well, I am in your thoughts. I have appeared to you at this time because of your great need, and I am here to assist you in conquering your world, slaying your enemies."

Walt stood silent and frozen. His mouth was gaping open.

"My name is Torakel. You may call me by my name, if you must."

It wasn't so much a voice, really. It seemed to be a whispery sound that came to him more through his mind than his ears.

Walt looked around the box for something moving or some way that sound or a signal could be coming from it. There was no speaker or opening, and the mouth sure as hell wasn't moving.

"Why are you examining me?" demanded the box, sounding offended, or maybe irritated. *"Have I been damaged? I do not sense damage. I have been preserved across centuries and I am indestructible. Many have tried and failed to destroy this sacred box."*

"Okay, okay, so if a box can talk, why here and… and why now?" Walt was beginning to think this was some kind of practical joke. He wondered if he'd ever mentioned his dream to anyone.

"I speak to you now as I have throughout time, to any who wish to rule by my side. You can claim the world and all that is in it, if you only trust in my desire to help you."

"Right, and where's the… the fine print?"

"You need only to feed my spirit, for my flesh is yet in waiting. Whatever you desire, you will simply speak it and it shall be yours. However, you must speak of it only to me."

Walt was bolder now. "What the fuck are you talking about? I still can't believe I am standing here talking to a box. Let's step back just 15 minutes ago, before the… your box was sitting on my table talking to me and shit. I mean, how did this happen, and why?"

"You sought me, Walt. I was unable to search for you."

"How do you know my name?" insisted Walt. "I've never seen you before."

"Oh yes, but you have. You saw me and now you have sought me. It is you who has sought me and brought out of the dark, and I who can provide you with what you are seeking. I will continue to speak to you until our time together is complete."

Walt paced back and forth in front of the table and thought back over his visions, his dreams. He could see that it *was* him who had searched for the box. What was the reason for that?

He felt a bit confused, but no longer frightened. In fact, he felt a little buzzed, as if he was filled with some kind of energy he had never experienced before.

"So what, you mean you grant wishes or something?"

"I can assist you in the fulfillment of your desires, yes, if that is what you mean. But…"

Walt suspected there'd be a 'but.'

"Before I can be of service to you, I need you to assist me. I must regain my strength. Your assistance will seal our agreement, and I shall be your servant."

"Oh man, you must be kidding me," said Walt, shaking his head. "All this time I've been barely squeaking by and I had a magic box, in a crate with my name on it!" It was the first time Walt smiled all day. "I think I'm losing it, no wait… I've lost it, but my brain doesn't know that it's gone yet. Yeah, I'm in shock or a coma or something, just like in those movies."

"Maybe I'm still passed out on the floor. Or maybe this is just a dream and, if I try, I can wake myself up." Walt slapped himself, hard in the face.

Shit, that hurts. He rubbed his cheek. *Definitely not asleep – must be nuts then.*

"Walt, you are no more insane than any other I have served. You have sought my presence and my assistance. We have work to do, and your world will not wait for you any longer. Your time to rule is at hand, but I need your help to make this so. You must provide me with what I need." There was a firm, almost impatient tone to the voice now.

"Oh, right. 'Fee-eed me.'" Walt used his best Little Shop of Horrors' talking, cannibal plant impersonation.

Ten

Monday morning arrived, and Walt went to work as usual. The strange box had not spoken to him since Saturday night, and he had begun to believe that the whole freaky incident had been just his imagination. He was actually a bit concerned that he might be losing his mind, but now that the episode was over, he hoped it was gone for good and life could be normal again.

When he sat down at his desk, he started up his computer. As he waited for it to boot up completely, he shuffled through some papers on his desk, tossing a few of the really old ones into the trashcan. Maybe all that clean up at home made him want to get rid of anything that wasn't current.

The computer booted up just fine and seemed to be working just fine this morning, of course. Wasn't that always the way? He didn't stop to think about it for long. It was going to be just another Monday.

Walt had been working for this company for three years now, a record for him. His jobs usually lasted about a year to a year and a half before something happened and he'd either get laid off or fired. It wasn't always his fault, but sometimes his short temper did get him into trouble. Somehow here he had avoided any unpleasant situations and stayed under the radar most of the time.

As a software support tech, his job was simply to wait until the phone rang, answer the call and help the caller solve their problems. Sometimes he thought this was the best job he ever had. Until last Wednesday, that is, when the boss called him into his office to give him that "special" assignment.

He had never before had to put together a spreadsheet for the boss, and he'd seen that as an opportunity to really demonstrate his chops and maybe even move up in the company. In fact, it had appeared that the boss was considering him for a possible management position. That is, if "bigger things in store" mentioned really referred to a promotion.

The spreadsheet he had worked on was created from data he had carefully collected from his co-workers, and it provided the sales and service statistics for the entire previous year. He had worked very hard on it, spending more than twenty hours on the research alone, and Walt was proud of the final result.

He was one of the first into the office as usual. Sometimes he enjoyed the quiet start, but sometimes it bothered him that his co-workers waited until the very last minute to arrive. Everyone else seemed so lackadaisical about his or her job, while he arrived an hour early nearly every day. Perhaps this was one reason he might be considered for a management position.

This morning, Walt was filled with great anticipation. He hoped that this was the day he'd get the credit he deserved for a job well done.

He clicked on the icon to open his email program, looked around waiting while he waited for it to open. While he was waiting, he heard Greg dragging himself through the door and into his cubicle. He was always so obnoxious in the morning, greeting everyone loudly as he made his way through the office.

"Mornin'," he called over the cube wall to Walt.

"Mornin'," came the reply.

Finally, Walt was able to check his email. There were 25 new emails, mostly customer questions and some spam. He clicked through them, deleting about two out of every three. He spotted the email he'd been hoping for, the one from his boss. Excitedly, Walt clicked on it.

Dear Mr. Turner,

I am sitting here at my desk wondering why a project that I assigned to you last week was completed and turned in by Mr. Owen. I gave you no direction or permission to re-assign the project to someone else. If I had wanted Mr. Owen to be responsible for the project, I would have assigned it to Mr. Owen directly.

Please place an appointment on my calendar to meet early Monday morning to discuss this further. Your future with this company could be at stake.

Thank you,

S. Palmer

Walt sat there, his mouth gaping, and reread the email. Did Palmer really think that Greg was intelligent enough to do all of the research on a project like that, let alone complete it? He was feeling sick to his stomach as he opened the calendar application and found a gap in Palmer's calendar around 9:30 AM. He filled in the body of the meeting, "To discuss project," and then blocked out the time. Robot-like, he entered Palmer's email address and clicked send.

Pushing back his chair, Walt got up and walked around to Greg's cube. He stood there staring at the back of Greg's head. He was just about to open his mouth to speak when Greg cut him off.

"Hey Walt… buddy… I got this weird email from Palmer… he said I did a great job on the project and wants to meet with me later today. Ain't that some shit? What the hell did you tell him?"

"Well, I guess he is referring to the fact that I used your computer to finish up that spreadsheet the other day. It went out with your email address. And, yeah, that *is* some shit!" said Walt with disgust.

"Wow, do you think he might give me a raise?" asked Greg. "I know they've been talking about promoting somebody to manager," he added. His face lit up with a smile.

"Greg, I can't talk about this right now. I'm too pissed off."

Walt turned away to go back to his desk. "Let me know what happens in your meeting. Palmer wants to meet with me too."

"Cool" replied Greg in his usual flip way. "Will do."

Walt sat down in his cubicle for the next half hour, staring into space and asking himself how this could have happened. If the economy were better and there lots of jobs and opportunities to choose from, he wouldn't worry so much about how this whole thing was going to go. But, at this point in time, lots of people were losing their jobs.

The next hour and a half clicked by slowly. Walt could overhear others in the office laughing and joking with each other. Some were talking about a new movie they had all seen over the weekend. Oh, how *good* it was!

Others talked about sports, their kids. Typical Monday morning office banter. Someone had gone fishing and caught an incredible amount of fish. *Good for them…* Walt thought, the clock ticking on, pounding in his brain.

Tick, tick.

As 9:30 drew closer, Walt's hands were beginning to sweat.

Tick.

Tick.

Tick.

9:29!

It was like an alarm going off in his head. He grabbed a stack of folders from his desk to prove to Palmer how much research and work he had put into the spreadsheet project. Maybe he could even convince him. Walt trudged down the hall to Palmer's office.

He rapped on the door. No answer. He could hear a voice coming from behind the closed door. There was a muffled, "come in," so he opened the door and stepped into his boss's office. The look on Palmer's face made him want to turn right around and leave. It was twisted up in a grim expression and flushed to a crimson color, not unlike a tomato. Walt could detect multiple large veins popping out on the older man's forehead.

Palmer was on the phone, and Walt could hear him saying, "Yes Ma'am… I know ma'am… sure, I'll handle that today… right… you know it!" Then he slammed the receiver down into its charger, and glared at Walt with bloodshot eyes.

"Mr. Turner," Palmer began. "Please explain to me how this spreadsheet project I assigned to you last week, the one I told you was so important… how did it get turned over to your neighbor, Mr. Walker?"

"Well, Mr. Palmer," Walt gulped. "The thing is… well, I was working on the spreadsheet Friday, putting the final numbers together so I could get it to you… and around three o'clock, my computer crashed…" Walt was squirming in his chair as he told the story.

"I had one of those 'Blue Screens of Death,' Mr. Palmer. You know what I mean? And I couldn't get the computer to reboot." Walt was afraid this wasn't sounding so good.

"So… I was talking to Greg about it… you know, I was trying to figure out what to do next… and Greg said I could use his computer to re-do the spreadsheet."

Now Walt could feel the sweat dripping as he continued.

"It took me a couple of hours to get the data from the server again," he said. A drop of sweat fell from the tip of his nose and landed on Mr. Palmer's desk.

"I finished it up right on time… just as you were coming back into the office. Really, Mr. Palmer, I was still working then, even after everyone else was gone. I finally finished it, but I didn't have any other way to get it to you quickly than to send it from Greg's email."

"I see," said Mr. Palmer. "So the spreadsheet really was done by you, not Mr. Walker?"

"No sir, I mean yes sir." *Maybe there's some hope,* Walt brightened a little.

"I did the research and completed it without any help from Greg, er… except, of course, I used his computer," Walt replied, sitting up straighter in his chair with a faint smile on his face.

Mr. Palmer cleared his throat. "Well, Mr. Turner, considering the circumstances, it's easy to understand how the mix up regarding the spreadsheet could have happened, but that does not begin to excuse the fact that we have a problem and action has to be taken to correct that problem."

"Problem sir?" Walt's heart was sinking again.

"Yes, Mr. Turner. When you came into my office you certainly noticed that I was on the phone?" Palmer squinted over his desk at Walt. "That was Alison Kramer, the CFO. She called to inform me that the figures you had provided were extremely inaccurate. In fact, they were off by about twenty percent!"

Palmer continued, his voice a little louder now. "Twenty percent lower than we had told our prospective new client. Now they've accused us of trickery, bait and switch as they called it, and they have chosen not to do business with us. To make a long story short, your mistake has cost us a ten million dollar contract!"

Mr. Palmer's voice seemed to trail off into an echo chamber, ten-ennnn mill-illion-ionnn doll-ollar-arrr con-ontrac-tractt!!!!

"Oh shit," was all Walt could get out as he suddenly felt the room begin to spin. "I-I don't understand, Mr. Palmer, I have all-all my paperwork right here. H-Hang on a minute, Mr. Palmer, let me just look at this..."

"'Oh shit' indeed Mr. Turner. Now I have other things to take care of here, and I really don't need to hear about how your computer ate your homework." Palmer said dismissively. He picked up the phone, punching three numbers. "Sherry, I'm ready for you now. Please come and show Mr. Turner out."

"You know, Walt," Palmer turned to him again. "I was thinking of writing you up for allowing Mr. Walker to finish the project I assigned to you, but now I regret to inform you that I've been asked to terminate our relationship."

Just then there was a knock at the door. "Come in, Sherry," said Palmer and motioned to Walt. "This is Mr.

Turner. He's a code 86, so please take care of it as quickly as possible."

Sherry looked over at Walt sitting there with his elbows on Mr. Palmer's desk, pale and shivering, burying his face in his hands. "Please come with me, Mr. Turner."

"Mr. Turner?"

Walt lifted his head to look at her, then slowly stood and followed Sherry to her office.

"Walt, I'm sorry. Let's try to make this as painless as possible," she whispered to him as they walked down the hall.

"How can this be painless?" he asked. "I don't even really understand how this is happening!"

As they reached her office, she motioned for him to go in first, and then shut the door behind them as she followed him.

Nearly forty-five minutes later, Walt walked back toward his cubicle carrying two large boxes, with Albert, the security guard, following right behind him.

"What happened, buddy?" Greg spoke in his usual overly cheery way. "Looks like somebody kicked you in the balls, and who's your new friend? You movin'? Dude, you get promoted?"

"I got fuckin' fired, *dude,*" Walt growled back. "And this shithead is here to escort me out of the building."

"Palmer can kiss my ass!" Walt added as he slammed the boxes down.

"Oh shit!" Greg stood up and peered over the cube wall. "Sorry, man. What happened?"

Walt was packing his collection of action figures into one box. "The spreadsheet was all fucked up, man. I don't know what happened."

He dropped one of his action figures on the floor. As he bent over to pick it up, he saw a sheet of paper lying on the floor under the filing cabinet by Greg's desk. He reached over, pulled it out, and looked at it. The heading at the top of the paper read, *Third Quarter Sales Projections.*

Suddenly Walt realized what had happened. When he was moving stuff from his cube to Greg's on Friday, this one very important paper must have fallen out of one of the folders. It was these missing numbers that had caused the spreadsheet to be out of whack by such a large percentage.

Walt stood up and leaned around the wall of the cubicle, he wanted to say something to Greg about the paper, but he seemed to be working on something important and he felt he better not interrupt. Then he decided to say something anyway, but not what he had initially thought to say.

He looked at Greg for a moment, then, "By the way, I think your meeting with Palmer may be cancelled. He thought you were the one who worked on the spreadsheet because I emailed it from your machine. Maybe he was going to fire you too!"

"Yeah, dude, I already got an email about it. But there is no reason for him to fire me, I didn't do anything."

"Yeah, I know. You are so perfect." Walt made a lewd gesture as though he was masturbating while glaring at Greg.

"Come on, man! I know you're pissed, but don't take it out on me. Hey, we should get together for a beer or something some time this week. We can talk about all this shit. I wanna hear how it went down."

The guard cleared his throat. "Come on, Mr. Turner. Cut the crap and let's get this over with." Albert kept his hand on his can of pepper spray in the holster on his belt as though Walt was a real threat.

Walt looked at him for a long moment. He felt an impulse to hit the prick with something, and instead turned back to finish loading the box. "Blow me," he muttered under his breath

Eleven

The whipped cream floating on his coffee had dissolved into a greasy sludge, and Walt continued looking out the window as if he were waiting for someone.

He'd stopped at the coffee shop on his way home and spent a considerable amount of time thinking about what he was going to do next. He had resigned himself to the fact that there were very few prospects for someone in this area.

This was a relatively small town after all. Most of the businesses were mom and pop stores or manufacturing facilities that didn't have much of a need for tech support personnel. With the state of the economy, there did not seem to be much opportunity anywhere these days.

Walt was thinking about the possibility of leaving here and maybe moving to a larger city where his skills might be more in demand. He decided to check into that as soon as he got home. For now, he was still looking out the window, and then down at the abandoned newspaper he'd picked up off one of the tables.

The front-page headline screamed, *Double Homicide Shocks Community*. Walt read the story about the man and woman who had been killed not far from where he lived. He marveled at the murderer's ability to live undetected in a small town, perhaps people who had lived here their whole lives. Perhaps he'd even passed them on the street or graduated with them from high school.

Walt didn't think that hiding in plain sight applied to small towns. In most small towns, everyone knows everyone else and everything about them. Walt felt lucky to enjoy a good bit of privacy and anonymity.

He was about to leave, then decided to look at the employment ads one more time before discarding the paper. There were ten or so ads, and he read them over again. When he was through, Walt laid the paper on the table and closed his eyes for a moment. He wondered what it would be like to just sell everything and leave here for a bigger city. Maybe even somewhere like New York City, or how about Atlanta? There must certainly be some work closer to one of those larger cities.

While he was sitting there with his eyes closed, darkness like a fog crept into his head. Walt began to make out the dark outline of something there in the shadows of his mind. It was the box. *"Come home, Walt,"* it whispered. *"Come home."*

Twelve

As he started up the stairway, Walt moved with some trepidation, not knowing what may be waiting for him inside the house. He wondered again if he was losing his mind, or did he have some kind of strange connection to the strange clay box.

He put his key into the door and turned it slowly, the click of the tumbler was louder than usual and it startled him. It seemed so quiet this afternoon. He couldn't even hear a bird chirping or a passing car. Maybe it was always this quiet here while he was at work.

He opened the door cautiously and stepped through it. Walt looked around the room. The box was still sitting on the table where he'd left it. The same blank look on it's face. Did he really expect it to be different? After all, it was just a piece of pottery. Fired clay and nothing more.

He walked over to the table and reached up to turn on the hanging light. He looked straight at the box, and said, "Yeah? I heard you tell me to come home, so what do you want?" Walt did not really expect an answer.

"Yes, Walt," the box replied, "We have much to do considering your situation. We must not waste the time we have now."

"What situation?"

"I am aware that you have suffered a great disappointment today, which has come to you at the hands of a man who never treasured the loyalty that you offer. I shall treasure your loyalty, Walt. You will find your devotion will be rewarded well."

"What do you know about my "great disappointment"? What the fuck is happening?" yelled Walt.

"Until today, this very moment in time, you have been the servant of a master who did not offer you riches and pleasure," the box replied, "but only scraps from his bountiful table, enough to hold you captive as his slave, to await your puny allotment given each month from his vast treasure. I have come to bring you out of that existence. I am doing this for you, with you, as a reward for your assistance and loyalty."

"So it was YOU who got me fired?!"

"No, I have not arranged for any harm to come to you. I can show you who sent you down this path, do you wish to see for yourself?" asked the box.

"So you know why this happened to me? All I know is that I screwed up really bad, and the chips fell all around me."

"Close your eyes, Walt, and the truth will be revealed to you, but I warn you, you will not be pleased."

"Oh, what the hell…" Hesitantly, Walt closed his eyes. He saw the scene in the office from Friday. It seemed to be the events shortly before his computer had crashed because someone was talking about their 2:30 coffee break. He could see into his cubicle, but he felt as though he was hovering over it.

Greg was there doing something to his computer, it looked like he was writing some code into it or something.

"There, that will fuck the weirdo up," said Greg, hitting the enter key on the keyboard, and then walking back to his own desk. He was whistling like he was real happy about something. What had he done??

Walt was now seeing himself walk back to his cubicle from the bathroom break he'd taken that afternoon. *Oh no,* now the replay of his computer crashing. He felt his heart pounding as he relived his reaction and the feelings of that moment. He saw Greg offering to let him use his computer and making a big deal out of it, like the fucker didn't know what was wrong!

He was about to witness the ultimate act of betrayal. He remembered that it had taken two trips with file folders to move everything he needed to finish the spreadsheet as he prepared to work in Greg's cube. Now as he watched, he saw what he'd been too upset to notice at the time.

Greg was checking around to see if Walt was looking, then he took a paper from one of the file folders and tossed it under his desk.

"Motherfucker!!" Walt yelled as he opened his eyes and found himself back in his apartment. "That fuckin' prick set me up to get fired! I'll kill his lying, treacherous ass!"

Walt focused again on the clay box. "How the hell did you do that? How could you show me something that happened when you weren't even there, and happened a few days ago? There is no way in hell you could have seen any of that."

"Walt, I have come from a far away time and place. I have helped more people to redeem their lives than you can ever count. I have come to serve you now, to offer you a reward for loyalty, for dedication. Just as I have rewarded others."

Walt hesitated. He thought about what he'd just seen, how Greg had set him up. He thought about how lonely his life had become since Mother had died, and how it seemed that everything sucked in his life. Not just right now, but for as long as he could remember.

Maybe this is my chance to change everything, he thought.

"Ok," Walt said aloud, "let's suppose you are real. How about explaining to me just what you are talking about. You don't have to give me all the particulars, just the important stuff, like... I don't know, the *important* stuff!"

"My spirit was called into this box many hundreds of years ago after I had met with Fate on the battlefield," said the box.

Walt sat down. It seemed like the box had a story to tell.

"Since that time, I have traveled long distances in the hands of men and women who have sought to fulfill their desires. I have rewarded their loyalty with great riches and power, and in turn they have provided me with what I need. I am very close to rebirth now, Walt. If you will assist me in this, I will bestow upon you the powers and riches I have promised, more than you are able to imagine."

"Well, Mr. Box... uh, I can't remember your name right now..."

"Torakel. Call me Torakel, if you must."

"Well, Mr. Torakel, when you say you have rewarded other people, what ever happened to them? What kind of people were they?" Walt's curiosity was piqued now.

"I have worked with leaders, artists, magicians and inventors. They were people like yourself, who in their time of need came into possession of this sacred vessel, and worked to fulfill my mission, in exchange for their well-deserved rewards."

"That sounds great, but what do I have to do to get this reward, the power and riches? What do you want from me exactly?" asked Walt.

"Spirits."

"Spirits?" asked Walt, sitting back away from the table.

"Spirits of those who will not be mourned or missed, the lost and the lonely… spirits of those whose future is undetermined. They are many in this world, and they drift through it like so much effluvia in the sea of life."

"Oh shit, really?" said Walt. "Spirits you say, is that all? How the hell am I supposed to give you spirits? Do I just walk up to someone and say 'Hey dude, I need to see your spirit for a minute,' and then snatch it and run? It doesn't sound like something a person could actually do. This is nuts!"

"It is much more simple than you know, Walt. You simply bring those lost people to me, and I will free them from their torments and allow them to be a part of something that is much greater than they could have been on their own."

"So how does that work?"

"You may remove my crown," replied the Spirit Box.

Walt leaned forward in his chair. The crown he had tried unsuccessfully to remove before now came off easily in his hands. He sat it on the table right next to the box. The blue glowing light that emitted from inside of the box instantly mesmerized him.

"As I have told you, many hundreds of years ago I was killed in a great battle," the box continued its story. *"My shaman had foretold that a sacred ritual would preserve my spirit until the day when I might be reborn. At the time of my death, my heart was removed and placed inside of this box along with my spirit."*

"So you are living inside of the box with other people?" Walt felt as though he were living out some fairy tale story. It made him feel silly for a moment.

"Look inside of the box, Walt, my heart still lives in wait of my rebirth."

Walt stood from his chair and cautiously leaned forward and peered into the box. The blue light glowed brightly from the bottom of the box, but there in the middle was a perfectly preserved human heart. So well preserved in fact, aside from its unnatural black color, Walt could have sworn that he saw it beating.

He sat down again slowly. "Is that your heart in there?"

"Yes, Walt, it is and it holds my spirit until I can be reborn. At that moment I will be free to pass into the body of another and live again to take my place as a powerful ruler in this world. With your help, I will achieve this and you will have the power to rule at my side for eternity."

"The shaman had explained that a multitude of spirits must join me here before I could be released. With each spirit that comes, I shall grow more powerful. Any who have dared to look inside of this box without my invitation have perished in this world and have joined their spirit with mine."

"You are special, Walt. In fact, you are chosen. And I have invited you to look upon my heart and allowed you to live so that you would trust me and understand that you must help me achieve my rebirth. I have waited for it these many centuries."

"Allowed me to live? That sounds threatening."

"I could have taken your life and your spirit the moment you removed my crown, but my plan for you is to be as my son, to rule with me by my side. Now you must help me to gather the spirits I require to live again. There is no time to waste, surely you must understand," replied the box.

"And just how do you expect me to go about this, is there some kind of spirit supermarket or something?" Walt asked sarcastically. "Come on, man! I've never even seen a spirit before. I don't know what to look for."

The Spirit Box replied, *"The spirit lives in the body before death, some may refer to it as the soul. Upon death of the body, the spirit passes on to a new level of awareness. I must have the spirit before it passes on. It is imperative that the exchange takes place directly. You must allow it to occur here, in this place."*

"You mean I have to bring people here and kill them, right here in my apartment?" Walt was getting pretty upset.

"No, I am not asking you to kill anyone. You simply bring them to me, and I will take what I need. Whatever is left of them will be easy for you to dispose of. There is already a place prepared to deposit the shells of my contributors."

"Contributors? This ain't no fuckin' charity we're talkin' about!" shouted Walt. "It doesn't sound like you're asking for *volunteers* exactly. If this means we're going to be killing people, I can get in some deep shit doing that! I don't want to go to prison for the rest of my life, or get my ass fried in the electric chair!"

"Would you like to live forever, rule your world, and have every pleasure you could ever imagine?" the Spirit Box persisted. *"When your work with me is finished you will never have to soil your hands again."*

"You'll probably just kill me when you're done with me." Walt suggested. "No, Mr. Torakel, Magic Box Man, I don't think I can do this. Besides how would I know who to bring to you? Anyway, I didn't ever soil my hands at work except when I changed the toner cartridge in the printer... No! This is starting to sound like some bat-shit crazy horror flick Greg would have told me about the day after he watched it."

"Yes... Greg... It was Greg that took from you the only means of your wealth. It was Greg who harmed you willingly and with great malice, as I have shown you. It is strange that you would mention him in such casual terms," replied the box. *"You would do well to bring him to me and allow me to repair the damage he did to you and to make right for what he has done to so many."*

"Well, based on the vision you showed me, Greg was more of an asshole than I knew, but I still don't know if that's enough reason to kill him. I mean, he was always playing practical jokes on people and no one ever killed him over it. You know it was Palmer who fired me, not Greg, right?"

"Perhaps you need to know this Greg better. People do not always portray themselves as their true nature. What do you know about his involvement with the woman?"

"His fiancée, you mean?"

"Close your eyes, Walt, and tell me if you think the woman would agree with you that Greg does not deserve to die."

Walt complied and closed his eyes. At first, it was difficult to focus on what he was seeing. These visions were always blurry as he entered them. Now he realized he was looking into a bedroom, he supposed that it must be Greg's apartment since Greg was coming out of the bathroom adjoining the bedroom. There was a woman lying on the bed sobbing. Her clothes appeared to be torn, and there were blotches of red on the sheet next to her. *Blood?*

Greg walked over to the side of the bed, stumbling a little as he crossed the room. He stood glaring down at her intently. "So, bitch, you think you can just do whate'er you want?"

He reached down and grabbed her by the hair, lifting her about a foot off the bed. He was obviously drunk and his speech was slurred. He twisted her head around so he could look at her face.

"Who wazzat fucker you were talking to tonight, huh? I betchyoo wished ya coulda gone home widdim! I should go back and kick *his* ass too!" he yelled, punctuating each phrase with a cold, hard slap to her face.

The woman recoiled from the blows, and Greg went into a rage. He ripped her blouse off with one hand and with the other grabbed the bed sheet beneath her and pulled hard, dropping her to the floor.

She screamed as he began kicking her in the stomach, the back, the shoulder and each time she tried to crawl away from him he would land another kick somewhere on her body.

Walt watched in shock as Greg continued to beat the woman until she lay there passed out. He called her a bitch before he sat down on the bed to catch his breath.

The scene was so real, it startled Walt. He opened his eyes and suddenly found himself back in his apartment, sitting at his table.

"What a fuckin' prick!" Walt cried out. "When was that? How long ago did that happen?"

"The time of this attack is of no consequence. This man, Greg, seems to do it often. How could you not wish to relieve him from this world? Would it not be merciful to all to rid him of whatever torment causes him to behave this way? And the torment he inflicts on others?"

"I don't care about whatever is tormenting him," said Walt. "All I saw was an abusive asshole and his helpless victim. Shit, maybe you're right. Maybe he does deserve to die, but how would I get away with something like that? Why should I be the one who has to do it? From watching that scene, I would think his fiancée would do it herself!"

"Get away with?" asked the voice in the Spirit Box. *"You don't have to get away from here with the remains after I take his spirit?"*

"No, no," answered Walt. "I mean, how do I bring him here to be one of your 'contributors' and not have someone know I have done this? If I get caught, I would probably spend the rest of my life in a prison somewhere."

"This Greg has no one who cares for him, no one would notice that he was missing."

The Spirit Box went on, *"When there is a problem that has gone unnoticed for years, and no one has cared enough to see the problem for what it really is – to see beyond what can be seen, then no one notices when the problem that was never recognized has been removed. Do you understand, Walt?"*

Walt was looking at the box in bewilderment. *What was this crazy ass Box trying to say?*

"Bring him to me, Walt. I will show you what can be done for the pain he has brought into this world. I will show you, Walt, the power that one day you may wield for yourself."

"So you *will* make an example of that asshole?" asked Walt.

"A demonstration of sorts, if you please."

Thirteen

When the phone in Greg's cubicle rang, he almost jumped out of his chair. He picked it up on the third ring.

"Hello, Greg Walker here..."

"Greg...dude...what's goin' on?" the voice on the other end said.

"Walt, is that you? Hey man, that really sucked, you getting fired and all. Turns out, Palmer cancelled my meeting with him after that and he hasn't even glanced my way since. Guess I'm nothin' special around here after all! I have no idea what is going on."

"Hey, man, that's kinda why I called," Walt replied. "I thought you might like to stop by my place later... uh, throw down a couple of beers or somethin'. I can fill you in on all the details... we can have a few laughs... uh, it'll be like a going away party."

Greg hesitated. Something in Walt's voice sounded a little off, and he really wasn't all that crazy about Walt. However, he was curious about how the whole firing episode went down. It might be a real kick to hear Walt's side of the story. Rumors around the office made it sound like Walt had actually broken down in tears and begged Palmer for his job.

"You okay, man?" Greg asked. "You sure you're up for company?"

"Yeah, I'm doin' okay. I'll figure somethin' out." Walt almost believed that Greg actually cared, except he had seen with his own 'eyes' what had really gone down.

"Okay, buddy, what time should I come by?" Greg figured he might as well take the opportunity to enjoy the little joke he'd played on Walt.

"Oh... um, I was thinking some time around six. I can order a pizza or something," said Walt.

"Sounds good," said Greg. "You live over that old antique shop, right?"

"Yeah, so you'll be here around six then?"

"Sure thing. Want me to bring anything? Maybe a six pack of your favorite, or something?"

"Nah, man... I'll take care of everything... I mean... all ya gotta do is show up. You're not going to believe what I got... uh, what I have here for ya." Walt was tripping over his words a little.

"Awesome," Greg said. "I guess I'll see you after work then. Later dude!"

Greg sat there a moment staring at his monitor screen. *Walt's sure a strange one,* he thought. The game of solitaire was still waiting for him, and best of all, he was winning for a change. So he went back to his game before the screensaver started.

Suddenly, he had a weird feeling, kind of a chill that went down his spine. Greg closed out the game and pushed his chair back from his desktop. He bent down and started looking under the desk for the paper he had thrown on the floor from Walt's folder.

He was planning on destroying the evidence, but he couldn't see it. He got down on his hands and knees, and felt around under the desk. The paper was gone.

He was beginning to wonder if Walt had discovered that he had messed with the folder. *No,* Greg assured himself, there was no way Walt could know. The cleaning crew that came in on the weekends probably picked it up. Besides, if Walt had found the paper on the floor, he probably would have blamed himself. He'd at least have said, "Shit!" if he'd found it.

"Shit" was Walt's favorite expression, Greg had learned after sitting next to him for a couple of years. He used to hear "Shit" coming from Walt it seemed like fifty times a day.

"Isn't that the shit?" he'd say when things went well.

"Shit!" when things sucked.

"What a bunch of shit!" whenever there was a new crisis.

No, even if Walt had found the paper, there was no way he'd connect it to Greg. Walt was just a guy with no real friends who wanted someone to talk to after getting fired. Since Greg was partly responsible for that, the least he could do was give Walt a shoulder to cry on – while he soaked up the glory for being such a clever fucker!

"Oh hell yeah!" said Greg with a measure of glee. "This is gonna be good!"

Fourteen

It was about a quarter after six when he heard footsteps coming up the stairs outside, then a loud knock at the door. Walt stood holding the door and looked at Greg standing there. For some reason, Walt couldn't think of anything to say just then, and felt his pulse quickening. He finally opened his mouth to invite Greg in when Greg spoke first.

"Dude, where's the can? I gotta piss like a racehorse!"

"Uh, over there," said Walt, gesturing. "Right off the bedroom."

Greg walked straight across the room without noticing the box. When you gotta go, you gotta go. Walt was relieved that he didn't have to talk about anything yet or answer any of Greg's stupid questions.

The box sat on the table where it had been since Walt discovered it. The crown lid was in place, so there was no unusual light in the room. Walt walked over to the refrigerator, got out two cold beers and sat them on the table, right next to the box.

It was so quiet in the apartment, that Walt could hear the sound of Greg peeing in the toilet. The toilet flushed, and Greg walked out of the bedroom.

"Nice place," he said, looking around. "I always thought your apartment up here would be like real creepy. You know, like deer heads and gargoyles and stuff… no offense, man… but this is like a real house. You sure have a lot of antiques. Hell, I bet some of this shit is worth a fortune!"

"A real house, huh? Yeah, I've always thought of it that way." *Greg is such a jerk,* Walt thought. "Anyway, come on over here to the table. I got you a nice cold Sam Adams here."

Greg was still looking around, touching everything. Picking things up, fiddling with them and examining closely before setting them back down. It was making Walt even more nervous.

He tried again. "I'll tell you all about my meeting with Palmer. I'm sure you're really gonna get a kick outta this."

Greg turned and walked over to the table. He reached for the beer and, immediately, the strange box caught his attention.

"Whoa," he said. "Now that's some awesome shit!"

Greg stood there admiring the box. He opened the bottle and took a long sip. "It looks like it's alive or something, man. That's the shit! You make that?"

Walt went back over to the kitchen to pull out some plates. He couldn't tell whether Greg was mocking him or not, but he wasn't about to give him the benefit of the doubt this time. He kept reminding himself about how nice and friendly Greg had sounded when he'd pulled that shit last week.

Greg kept on jabbering away about Walt's apartment while Walt was remembering the scene with Greg's fiancée. Walt could feel his hands start to clench.

"Tell him to remove my crown," Walt heard the voice.

"Not yet, man," whispered Walt between his teeth, glaring at the box.

"What'd you say, dude?" Greg asked. He reached out and ran his hand over the face on the box, slowly tracing the features with the tips of his fingers.

"I just said, 'Oh, yeah.' I inherited that box from my mom. I think it might be made with real gold. I'm not sure." He stepped closer to Greg and bent down to look at the box as if to check it out.

"Whoaa…. I bet that shit is worth some cash! If those spikes are solid, there must be half a pound of it there."

Greg couldn't remember what the current price of gold was but, judging by the material the box was made of, and the price he guessed that the gold might be worth, he estimated that the box could be worth a fortune. A sparkle began to shine in his eyes.

"My crown must be removed before I can do what must be done," Walt could hear the voice say. *"You must find a way."*

Greg thought maybe he could knock Walt out and slip out without being seen or…

"I know!"

Walt's voice penetrated Greg's thoughts. He looked over at Walt, who was standing a little too close for Greg's comfort.

"Uh, I mean… I know you wanted to hear what happened with Palmer… what they said when they were firing me and all. Ya know, at first he thought you had done the spreadsheet project instead of me. That was why he sent you the email. At first, I thought he was going to give you a raise or something, maybe that promotion everyone has been spreading rumors about."

"Here, take a seat," Walt pulled out the chair next to Greg and another one for himself. They both sat down with Greg seated directly in front of the box.

"I told Palmer what happened with my computer, and how you let me use yours to finish it up… uh, I didn't know if it was making me look better, or you. I was just tellin' the truth to set the story straight."

Walt took a swallow of beer and continued. "Man, someone was on the phone with Palmer, when I got in there… it turns out it was the CFO tellin' Palmer that the numbers on the report were all fucked up. Somehow, I fucked up and left some numbers out and the figures were pretty far off. So guess what? We lost a ten million dollar contract because my numbers were so far off. Then he fired me."

"Wow," said Greg. "That really sucks. I sure am glad you cleared up who'd really done the spreadsheet. I mean… sorry, bro… I can't help it. I'm glad it wasn't my fault."

"You know what *really* sucks?" Walt's eyes were a little bugged out now. He wanted to tell Greg the he knew that it *was* Greg's fault, but he decided against it just now.

"What *really* sucks is that I've had that job for quite a few years and I wasn't even vested in my retirement plan yet. I was even starting to like Kathie, and I thought I might have had a chance with her."

"Well, dude, just because you lost your job doesn't mean you can't go out with Kathie and give her a little bonefish if you know what I mean, huh?" Greg reached over and slapped Walt's shoulder and laughed, a little too heartily at his own little joke.

Walt gritted his teeth. "I don't know about that," he said tightly. "It took a long time for me just to get up the nerve to talk to her in the first place. I was almost at the point of asking her out when I got fired. Now I'm not sure how I'm ever gonna get that chance."

"Man, you are such a pussy, dude. You shoulda already had her by now. Hell, you'd probably be living in this apartment with a couple of kids right now! A couple of fuckin' brats, prob'ly." Greg had another chuckle and then a swallow of beer. He was starting to wonder if Walt had ordered the pizza.

"Oh yeah, right, and they'd probably be drawing on the walls and shit, right buddy?"

"Only if you let 'em," nodded Greg smiling back at Walt who was, for some reason, beaming at him with a grin of his own. There seemed to be something strange about the way Walt was looking at him.

Walt rose out of his seat. "But really, Greg, all kidding aside," he chuckled at his pun, "what really sucks about the whole getting fired thing is what I found out after that."

Walt reached toward the box and lifted off the crown. It gave off something like a mist and the blue glow Walt had seen before. It almost looked like a thick swirling flow of blue liquid rising upward toward the overhead light.

Greg was sitting in his chair, mesmerized by the blue light coming from the box as the thick mist began to flow across the table toward him.

"I found out you did something to my computer to make it crash that day," Walt said as he set the crown carefully on the table. "You also removed one of the papers from my folder and hid it under the desk."

Greg barely acknowledged that he had heard him, he was still focused on the blue swirl of light coming closer.

"Oh, yeah, ya shithead. I found it when I was packing up my shit." Walt took two steps back from the table, glaring at the back of Greg's head.

"And it was because of you I got fired, you fucking prick!" He felt a vein start to throb in his forehead as he yelled.

Greg still didn't turn around... Instead, he reached down with both hands and grabbed the edge of the table as if he were going to pull himself up from his seat.

Walt could see his fingertips compress against the edge of the table. Greg was holding on so tightly that blood began to seep from around his fingertips, but he didn't seem to be able to let go. When Greg's fingers pushed far enough down that his fingernails came in contact with the wood, they shattered completely. A look of pain and fear shot across Greg's panicked face.

Walt couldn't stop watching despite the horror he was feeling.

Greg's wild man eyes began to bulge from their sockets. He was moaning softly, swaying a little, and the pitch of his voice was rising higher and higher. He began to shake violently, still gripping the edge of the table with beyond human strength. Walt wanted to shut out the sounds of bones cracking as Greg's fingers broke into odd angles.

Walt could see Greg's head tilt back, his mouth opening wider than any human jaw should allow. A hissing, shrieking scream escaped from his mouth, and a translucent likeness of Greg's face suddenly materialized from his now dangling jaw, bursting out from it with a loud "POP." The apparition hung there in front of its owner as though attached by a ghostly, elongated neck.

Suddenly Greg broke his grip from the table, and as if trying to catch a puff of smoke between his hands, he clawed at the air as more and more of his spirit oozed and squeezed out through his jaws away from his shuddering body.

With each fraction of a second, the blue light coming from the box grew brighter. It was blinding to Walt, desperately trying to cover his eyes, yet still trying to see what was happening.

Nothing could have prepared Walt for such a strange and unnatural event. His eyes were locked as prisoners on the terrible sight. It was a compulsion beyond the impulse to look at a tragic accident on the freeway.

Inch by inch, Greg's spirit left his body. His eyes widened in panic and helplessness. As the spirit neared the opening of the box, it seemed to hover there for a moment, oscillating from side to side as though struggling to free itself from Greg's body. Walt could see that the spirit was caught by its "feet," hung up at the lower jaw.

A rush of wind seemed to come from nowhere, and Walt could hear a loud snapping sound like a tree shattering in a storm. The spirit at last broke free from Greg's body and was sucked into the box.

Walt stood motionless as the lid from the box lifted from the table where it had been placed, levitating to a position above the box, and landed exactly in position. The light, the wind, and Greg's spirit were gone.

All that remained was the smell of ozone in the air and the remainder of the mist settling to the table.

Finally, Walt could look away and he moved immediately to look at what was left of Greg's body, slumped over on the table. He staggered and collapsed to the floor. "Oh shit, oh shit!" he cried. "What the fuck was that?"

Fifteen

Walt stared in horror at Greg's shriveled corpse. It appeared much smaller now, dried up like a giant prune, and about the same color. There was a vaporous wisp rising from the body as though it had been flash dried in a kiln or even struck by lightning.

"You didn't tell me it was going to be like that!" Walt yelled at the box with his arms wildly gesturing. "You could have fucking warned me or something!"

"Would you have gone through with this if you had known?" asked the box.

"Probably not." Walt and the Spirit Box spoke the same answer.

"That was fucked up-*up*." The box finished the word "up" at the same time it left Walt's lips.

"What the hell, can you read my mind too?"

"Many have asked that same question, Walt. Do you believe that your thoughts and feelings are so much different from others who have experienced my power for the first time? Most of the others wretched as they witnessed it…"

Walt had much to learn. He was pretty shaken up, and he'd hate to admit anyone that he was scared shitless by what he had just seen.

"Do not fear, Walt, you have helped me. Now I will reward you. What is it that you desire from me?"

"How do I know I won't end up the same way? What's keeping you from doing that to me?"

"You can be assured, Walt. No harm will come to you."

"Easy for you to say."

Walt turned away and considered the opportunity before him. The offer turned over in his mind, and he turned back toward the box.

"If I tell you what I want, do you just make it appear like some kind of wizard?" asked Walt.

"Yes."

"Well, if that's really the case, how about those riches you keep talking about? I want that."

"As you say," replied the box. *"Where shall I place it?*

"Uh… In the bedroom!" Walt prepared himself for disappointment.

Immediately, a light shone from the bedroom doorway, and Walt crossed the room quickly to see what had happened. There on the bed was a pile of valuable objects. He rubbed his eyes and walked in to get a closer look. There were stacks of hundred dollar bills, gold coins and precious gems set in fine jewelry: necklaces, bracelets, rings and earrings. There were various art objects including jeweled eggs and boxes encrusted with gold and jewels.

Walt was amazed at the mound before him and wondered at its incredible value. He picked up one of the necklaces to examine a tag attached to it. The tag read, "Fontaine's Jewelers." He dropped the necklace on the bed and stormed back into the living room.

"That fuckin' jewelry is from the fuckin' store down the street!" Walt screeched, feeling betrayed and fearing the cops might pull up anytime. "Shit! I mean, why'd you steal it from the store right down the street?" He was walking around looking out the windows, then closing the blinds.

"I am not a goldsmith, nor am I a jeweler. I cannot make your riches appear without a source. I can create organic objects from nothing, but not inorganic. I simply bring those objects to you from their closest source."

"How about the money? Where'd it come from then?" Walt was still pacing.

"The paper-gold came from a building where men holding weapons were watching over it. It must have great value to warrant such protection. There were men in cages there as well, perhaps slaves waiting to be sold."

"What are you talking about? Slaves?!" exclaimed Walt as he ran back into the bedroom and picked up a stack of the bills. As he flipped through it he looked at the serial numbers. Sequential! This must have been money used by the cops, maybe for a drug buy or something! Marked money! "Shit!!"

He ran back to the table with a stack of the bills in his hand and stood there glaring. "None of this stuff is any good to me," he said shaking the money at the box. "I mean, sure, it is great riches just as you promised, but I can't sell or spend any of it. I'd end up in jail! Right next to the 'slaves!' "

"Perhaps your desires are misguided, Walt. Many assistants throughout the centuries have asked for power rather than riches, for with great power comes great reward. I can give you power Walt. Simply ask for it."

"A politician spends millions of dollars to get elected to a job that only pays about a hundred thousand a year. Maybe he's got that same idea. But this is bullshit! Fuckin' look at

Greg's body, man! What the hell am I supposed to do with that?"

"You do have some space below in your shop, do you not?" asked the box. *"You can store the remains of my contributors there until our work is finished. After that, it will make no difference."*

"You keep talking about *our* work and *it* being finished. Just when would what be finished?" asked Walt.

"Before you searched for me, I sat dormant there, in need of four spirits. Now you have provided one and I only require three more, and then the vessel. When my needs have been filled, your work will be complete and our power will be made whole."

"The vessel, the vessel? You keep saying 'the vessel.' What is this vessel?" replied Walt.

"The vessel is the body through which I will be reborn. It is the reason we have been united in this time, so that you may assist me and rule by my side upon my rebirth."

"Uh, right… We'll discuss this later," said Walt. "I'm moving Greg downstairs, then I gotta figure out where I'm gonna hide him."

Sixteen

Walt was restless most of the night and only slept fitfully off and on. His mind kept playing Greg's death over and over like a video loop with no pause button. *That was some weird shit!*

Finally, after taking a sleeping pill from his mother's old medicine cabinet, Walt fell into deep and dreamless sleep. No surprise there, since all of his nights were dreamless since he had carried the strange box up from the shop.

Late the next morning, he awoke with a slight headache. He walked to the medicine cabinet, still open as he had left it, and retrieved a couple of ibuprofen capsules from an out of date bottle. Tossing them back into his throat, Walt leaned over the sink and gulped some water from the faucet to wash the pills down.

Walt went back into the bedroom and sat on the bed, thinking about everything that had happened the night before. He couldn't remember moving the money and jewelry from the bed before he'd climbed in. He looked around the room trying to remember where he'd put them, but they were nowhere to be seen.

He stood and walked into the living room and yelled over toward the Spirit Box. "Hey, what happened to my money and jewelry?"

There was no answer. *Do spirits sleep?* He wondered.

He walked over to the table and sat down looking at it. He was tempted to knock on it to see if he could get a response. After a few minutes, he asked again. "What happened to all the treasure from last night?"

"The treasure did not please you, Walt, so I disposed of it to eliminate the problem."

"Since you 'eliminated the problem,'" Walt sounded irritated, "how are we going to replace my reward?"

"Your wish and desire has been fulfilled. I'm not able to invoke a replacement for your reward. Your next request will be granted once I have received a new spirit."

"Oh, great," whined Walt. "Last night you added Greg to your spirit collection and, what? All I got was this lousy T shirt!"

"T what? I do not understand."

"Never mind, it's just a saying!"

"I see, a saying, and you were saying it, so it must be said. We need to continue with our work, Walt. Time is growing short!"

"Time is short, now? You told me you have been working this plan for centuries and now you want to be in a big hurry?"

"Yes, we must act before the moon is next a full round, or we will be forced to wait another cycle."

"But the full moon is only a few days away! How many spirits do you need before then?"

"I must have but three more spirits and then the time will come to seek out the vessel for my rebirth. Time is short and they will come for you if we hesitate."

"Huh? Who will come for me? What the fuck? I don't want to go to prison for murder!" said Walt as he felt all the blood rushing from his limbs and his head spinning as he considered how he might explain away a shriveled crust of a body in the shop downstairs.

"You are not suspected, at least not yet," the spirit assured him, *"but after some time, the friends of your co-worker will contact someone about his disappearance. If we wait until the next moon, we will need to leave this place to finish our work for it will become too dangerous. It will become difficult to accomplish what we must do somewhere else, when we can easily finish it here."*

"Okay already, I forgot even assholes like Greg have friends, and he still had *his* job so they will be looking for him there, too, I suppose. So what am I supposed to do for your next meal? Kidnap a paperboy? How about a German shepherd?"

"There is no time to travel to Germany, Walt. I have already explained why we must find the spirits I need here. A shepherd would do, but have never known of any in this region."

"Are you really so fucking stupid? I wasn't talking about a person! Man, a German shepherd is a big dog."

"A dog does not have the sort of spirit I require. I have been presented with dogs in the past, and these creatures have exploded as their spirit began to leave their body."

"Well, that settles one question of modern religion, I guess. A lot of people don't believe that dogs actually have a spirit, but now I know they do. Remind me not to bring that up in public. So got any ideas where I should get you your next meal then? It is kind of tricky to kidnap people these days."

"There is a place where you go for your food. The sign says D-I-N-E-R. There will be a woman there in one hour, a woman with crimson

hair. She is looking to speak with someone about her deep feelings. You will be the one she seeks. You will bring her here."

"And you think she'll just come home with a stranger? Right! I guess you think I'm some kind of a chick magnet? I've never even been able to get a woman to go out on a date! How the hell am I going to get one to come here?" Walt was gesturing around him.

"You will ask her to join you as you eat. You will tell her she looks as though she has a secret to share. When you finish your food, you will offer to bring her here and drink ale, and she will come. It will happen as I have said."

"You can see it, right? You see the future? What am I hiding behind my back?" asked Walt as he took his hand from behind his back and flipped his middle finger in the direction of the box.

There was to be no reply. There was apparently nothing more to say. The Spirit Box was waiting. Walt walked over and sat down on the sofa.

Seventeen

Detective Hazard pulled his unmarked car into the parking lot of the Mainline tavern. It was not yet noon and already there were ten cars in the parking lot. He grabbed a folder from the passenger seat and got out of the car, slamming the door as he walked toward the door.

The Mainline had been around awhile. First opened in the Seventies, it had been quite a hangout in the early days. It was quite dark and dingy inside and was defined by the old signs and memorabilia that decorated the walls. It was one of the few bars in the state that still allowed smoking *indoors*. In the old days, the Mainline was the place to go for shows by young, up-and-coming rock bands. But now the stage was empty, decorated only with few artificial plants and a large cardboard standup of Steve McQueen.

The favorite joke at the Mainline was played on new patrons. The restroom doors were marked with custom-made signs on the restroom doors. On the men's room door, there was a large hand pointing at the ladies' restroom and on the ladies' restroom door there was a similar sign pointing at the men's restroom. Regulars at the bar would spend part of the night watching as a new customer, looking for the restroom, would walk into the room assigned to the opposite sex. Realizing their mistake, they'd run out red-faced, and hurry into the appropriate side.

John remembered the first time he'd done this. That wasn't so bad, but he was ashamed to admit that sometimes still he found himself lingering outside the restrooms, trying to remember which one he was supposed to use.

These days, the Mainline was known as a pickup place for middle-aged women and younger guys who were looking for an easy lay. A few workers leftover from the graveyard shift could be found there the mornings chatting with the diehard drinkers, none who would ever admit to being an alcoholic.

John walked up to the bar and slid onto one of the barstools. Alex walked over to him, wiping the bar with a towel. The bartender smiled, "What can I do for ya, detective?"

John was a regular here, but not so often as a customer. Most of the time, he came here looking for information to solve the petty crimes that were common to most boring little towns. In fact, the Mainline was usually the first stop when the clues did not all line up.

"Well, Al, I've got a bigger deal here than usual. This time it's a double homicide…"

"You mean murder in this town? Damn! Was that on the news?"

"Yeah, I'm going to need you to take a look at a few photos. I'm not sure if the story broke on the news yet, I don't get to watch much." He opened the folder and laid two photos on the counter. The first was a picture of Todd standing with a girl next to a giant ball of twine and a sign that read "World's Largest Ball of Twine."

The other photo was Todd's fiancée, Sara. This one looked like a graduation photo about five or so years earlier. John surmised by looking at the photo that this girl was a total bitch, but that was no reason for someone to kill her. Especially that way.

Alex examined the photos for a minute or two, tapping his finger on the bar. "I don't recognize the girl, but this one looks like this guy named Todd. He comes in here pretty often."

"Todd." John repeated, and scribbled the name in his folder. "Do you know his last name?"

"No. Is he a suspect?"

"I was just curious how well you might have known him. I need to know, have you seen him recently?"

"Well, whoa, wait a minute, wasn't Todd the guy who was murdered the other night? Geezus!" Alex face brightened and he was pleased with himself for being up on current events. "They didn't give the names out on the news yet, did they? That's Todd for sure."

"Like I said, I don't follow the news, but you are correct, his name is Todd," replied John, a bit troubled by Alex's enthusiasm. "Did you see him here with anybody?"

"Oh, hell yeah. He left with that Rachel chick. She looked pretty blasted and she was leaning and hanging onto him when they left."

"Do you know her, uh, Rachel's, last name?" John asked, scribbling again in his folder.

"Most people pay with plastic these days, so I get a look at their names on their card when I run a tab for them. But Rachel, she never uses a card; only cash, if she even pays for her own drinks. I only know her first name cause the guys are always talking about how they had a piece of Rachel last week, or last night. Too many to count."

"Is there anyone here right now who you think might know her last name or where she lives?"

"No, not right now, but if you come in after six, there are probably ten or fifteen guys who might be able to clue you in on that."

"Thanks, I'll do that. How about giving me a description of her?"

"Well, she's got red hair and kinda pale skin. She's about up to here on me," Alex held his hand just below his chin, "and she has a *really* nice ass!"

"Is that all you can recall? 5', 5", red hair, pale skin, and a nice ass?"

"Green eyes, damn, but I love green eyes! That's all I got for ya right now, though," said Alex.

"Ok, then, I guess I'll have to come back later. Around six, you said?"

"Yeah, man, I'm sure you'll get what you need then."

John picked up the photos from the bar, slid them into the folder and walked out.

"Dude," Alex yelled after him. "You didn't tell me what happened! Who was the girl? She looked like a total bitch!"

John replied with one word over his shoulder.

"Later."

Eighteen

When Walt arrived at the Big T Diner, Rachel was just being served a plate piled with fries and a burger. Walt walked through the door and called out, "Hey, T, what's going on?"

From behind the counter, T replied, "Not much yet, man, but if you see it comin' be sure to let me know, cause it's the same old shit today all day." He smiled over at Walt and got back to work cleaning the cabinets.

Walt stood by the counter for a minute and looked at the red-haired woman in the giant mirror on the wall. She looked haggard, like she hadn't slept for a week, and there were dark sagging folds of skin beneath her eyes. He took a breath in, gathering his courage, and then stood up.

He walked over and looked right at Rachel, hesitating there trying to recall what it was that he was supposed to say. Finally, he remembered what the Spirit Box had told him.

"Hi… mind if I sit with you? You look like you need someone to talk to."

Rachel was picking at her fries. She looked up at Walt with a puzzled expression. "Strange that you would say that, I was just sitting here thinking how nice it would be to have someone to talk to." Picking up her burger, she took a small bite. She nodded and waved at the seat across from her.

"Yeah, you look like you've got some kind of secret to share or something," He said, easing, himself into the booth.

"What'll ya have today, Walt?" asked T.

"I'll have what she's having," Walt replied and sat looking at her for a moment. "So, my name is Walt and you are?"

"Rachel," she replied as she took another bite from her burger, chewing it slowly. "Tell me something about yourself, Walt. I don't know anything about you."

"What do you want to know? Go ahead, ask me anything."

"Well… do you come here often?"

"Yeah, I'm in and outta here all the time." Walt was leaning back in his seat with his arms folded in front of him. "Okay, so ask me something a little more off the wall."

"Well, I don't know about 'off the wall,' but… okay… Have you ever done something really bad and you were scared to death you'd get caught?"

Walt smiled over at her and shrugged. "Sure hasn't everyone?" I mean, I cheated on a test once. I thought for sure the teacher would figure it out."

"No, Walt… I'm talking about something really bad, like go-to-jail bad," she said, her voice lowering into a conspiratorial tone.

Walt leaned forward and squinted over at Rachel wondering what she was hiding.

"It's not like I really meant to do something bad," she went on. "In fact, it was an accident… were you ever in a situation where something really bad happened, and it was an accident, but it looked like you planned to do something bad. I mean, to someone who didn't see the accident happen, it looked intentional?"

"Whoa!" Walt leaned back in his seat again. He wasn't exactly sure where this was going. "This sounds serious. Maybe you want to tell me exactly what happened."

She stared down at her fries and began, "Well, I was at the Mainline the other night and I met this guy…" She stopped talking abruptly as T walked over holding Walt's burger and fries.

"Need ketchup and a Coke, too, T." said Walt, salting his fries before he turned back to Rachel and continued. "Sorry, go ahead."

T came right back with a bottle of ketchup and a cold drink, setting them on the table in front of Walt. "Here ya go," he said as he pulled out a straw from his pocket and laid it down in front of Walt. "Anything else?"

"No thanks," Walt smiled and waved him away while Rachel stuffed a couple of fries into her mouth.

He picked up the straw and began peeling the paper off. He shoved it into his drink and picked up the ketchup bottle, flipping open the lid with his thumb. Walt squeezed about a quarter of the bottle on his plate.

"I love ketchup." He laughed. "In fact, the only reason I eat fries is because it's kind of rude to suck ketchup right out of the bottle."

She smiled again. "Hey do you have any plans this afternoon?" Walt asked. "I gotta twelve-pack at my place and I don't have any plans. If you want to come over and talk some more, maybe you could get to know me enough to tell me your story? You'd probably feel a lot better if you got it off your chest."

She looked as though she might say no before she responded, "Yeah that sounds good, I think I could use a beer or two, or six! Let's eat this and then go."

Walt thought to himself, *How easy was this? All these years this is all I had to do to meet women?* He'd have to remember exactly what he'd said to her, and maybe try it again soon with someone he wasn't planning to kill.

Kill? Ugh, I mean feed to the box. I'm never going to go through with this unless I can think of it that way.

He wolfed down his burger to catch up with her, and was soon wiping his mouth with the paper napkin and asking T for the check. "I'll pay for yours," he said to Rachel, who was digging around in her purse.

"Thanks, man. I owe you one." She closed up her purse and pulled the strap up over her shoulder.

Walt laid a twenty-dollar bill on the table and they were walking out the door together. "Where'd you park?" asked Walt.

"I don't have a car. I usually walk or take the bus when I go out."

"Me too," said Walt. "We're lucky my place isn't too far from here. I guess we'll walk off some of that burger."

When they were almost there, Walt turned into the alley to climb the stairs along the side of the building before Rachel asked, "You live above the old antique shop?"

"Yeah, the shop was my mom's when she was still alive. She died about a year ago".

"I'm so sorry," she said. "I didn't know. I thought the shop had gone out of business. I used to stop in there once in a while and always ended up buying something. To tell you the truth, when I'd get it home sometimes, I'd wonder why I wasted my money. I mean, I just felt like I couldn't live without it for some reason. Until I got it home, that is."

"Really?" said Walt as he turned the key in the door and opened it. "Well, the place is mine now."

They stepped through the door and he flipped on the light. "Go ahead and have a seat at the table," he said. "I need to use the bathroom."

Walt's pulse was quickening as he crossed the living room to his bedroom door. He kept thinking about Rachel's fate as she takes a closer look at the box sitting there. He had no idea how it was going to go this time, he just wanted it over with. He walked through the bedroom to the bathroom and closed the door behind him.

Walt leaned against the door with his eyes squeezed shut. He thought his heart was going to explode through his chest as he waited for the screams that didn't come. He waited for a minute or two before he flushed the toilet and ran some water in the sink pretending to wash his hands.

He went out and walked back through the bedroom to the living room area and looked over at the table where Rachel was sitting, looking at the box.

"This is a really cool box; the face looks kind of spooky, but I like spooky." Rachel ran her fingers around the features on the face. "Does the lid come off? What do you keep inside it?"

"Uh... sure the lid comes off. Go ahead and see for yourself," said Walt.

"I'll get you a beer," he said as Rachel lifted the lid and set it on the table. Walt headed for the refrigerator. Now he was really getting nervous. He didn't actually have a twelve-pack, just three beers leftover from when Greg was over. What if the box was going to ignore him and drag this thing out?

He opened the refrigerator door and looked at the beers on the shelf just as he heard Rachel saying, "What the...?

That looks like some kind of body part in there, like a heart or something. Yuck, that's disgus…"

Walt turned to see what had happened just in time to see the blue light beginning to fill the room. Rachel was standing there bent over the box. Her mouth was still open as if the words had frozen on her lips. Her hands were resting on the tabletop and she began to shake slightly, then faster and more intensely.

She turned her head to look at Walt, and he saw the terror in her beautiful green eyes. There was a look of extreme pain on her face when suddenly her head snapped back to look directly into the box. Her mouth began to open wider, so wide Walt could hear her jaw cracking as it broke, and then her mouth opened wider still.

Rachel was still upright, shaking violently now, as her spirit began to separate from her body. Walt watched as it stretched and pulled toward the opening of the box. It looked just like Rachel, but transparent and pale.

Suddenly with the cracking sound of a splintering tree, her spirit broke loose from her body and flew into the box. The lid levitated, quickly lifted and placed itself on top of the box.

The dried and shriveled shell of her body fell away and forward, and her head hit the table hard with a thud. It shattered like a piece of pottery into dusty pieces that flew in all directions as the rest of her fell to the floor.

Walt ran to the sink and threw up, still holding two bottles of unopened beer in his hands. The ketchup he had consumed less than an hour ago now burned in his sinuses. He heaved a couple more times before he finally straightened up and wiped his mouth on a hand towel he took from the counter.

He set one of the beers down and twisted the cap off the other one. Taking a long gulp to wash down the bitter taste in his mouth, Walt walked over to the table. He stood there looking at the headless shell of Rachel's body lying on the floor and the pieces of her head scattered everywhere as the dust settled around them.

"It will get easier, Walt. There are only a few more spirits to collect, and then it will no longer be necessary to find those who can contribute," said the box. *"We are close to our destiny, and you will want for nothing ever again."*

"Shit, this is disgusting, how many times have you done this crazy spirit stealing thing to people before? Doesn't it bother you, killing a woman like that?"

"I have taken the spirits of young and old, strong and weak, man and woman, beauty and beast. The number of 'how many' escapes me, but I know what remains, and three more must give themselves to me before I can be reborn."

"Now please tell me how I may reward you," urged the box.

Nineteen

It was 6:15 exactly when John pulled into the parking lot of the Mainline Tavern. He grabbed a notepad and the case folder off the seat before stepping out. He could hear the crunch of gravel from beneath his shoes as he walked to the door of the bar.

As he pushed the door open and stepped inside the bar, every head turned at once to look at him. Ironically, the jukebox began to play "Superstition", and everyone turned back to their drink or conversation.

He walked over to the bar where Alex was washing up a sink full of glassware. "Hey Alex, gimme a draft, will ya?" he said.

"Sure thing, John. You off the clock?" asked Alex.

"Unfortunately, in my line of work, there really isn't a clock. Just work, all day and all night, phone calls when I'm trying to sleep, and nobody at home to bitch at me after dark. Anyway, I'm hoping to talk to some of those guys we talked about earlier. Any of 'em here?"

Alex tilted the beer glass to let the foam drain off as he filled it. "Only one", he replied. "I hear there was a problem over at the plant earlier and some of the others will be working late. Wanna talk to the loner?"

"Sure, let me put this beer away first then you can introduce me." He tilted the glass back and finished nearly all of it in three swallows, paused, exhaled, and finished the rest.

"OK," John said as he set the glass down on the bar and wiped his mouth with the back of his hand. "Let's get the party started."

Alex walked from behind the bar wiping his hands with a towel and John followed him to a booth against the wall. There was a dark-haired guy, somewhere in his mid-thirties, sitting with a beer and two empty shot glasses. "Yeah, what's up?" he asked when he saw John.

Alex answered, "Joey, this is Detective Hazard. He's investigating that murder that was on the news the other day. You know, the couple found dead? He wants to..."

"Just a couple of questions, if that's OK?" John finished, flashing his badge.

"Sure, no worries. I ain't done nothin'," said Joey.

From the folder he was carrying, John pulled out Todd's photo and laid it on the table in front of Joey. "Do you know this guy?" He tapped on the photo and watched Joey's reaction.

"Oh hey, that's Todd. Haven't seen his lame ass since he left here with some chick, Rachel, the other night. Wanted to ask him how it went, know what I'm saying?" said Joey.

"So you saw him leave with someone named Rachel… Do you know where they were going?" asked John.

"I'm pretty sure they were headed to Todd's place. In fact, it was pretty weird cause Todd's girlfriend came by about twenty minutes after they left, and she was looking for him. She ain't never come here before. Whoa, you mean that bitch killed Todd and Rachel?" said Joey.

"Did Todd's girlfriend talk to anyone while she was here? What'd you say her name was?" asked John.

"I never caught her name, but, yeah, she talked to a guy who was sitting at the bar. Sorry, man, I really don't know his name either," said Joey.

John scratched some notes on his pad. He sat there looking at them for a minute or so before he continued, "Do you know anything about this Rachel? Know where she lives?"

"Yeah, she lives over on Maple Street, about a half block from the corner of King, it's the only yellow house in that block. Uh, actually I've never been there myself, but a friend of mine has," he said, trying to hold back a smile.

"What's this 'friend's' name?" John asked.

"Alejandro." He hesitated, then, "Hey, he isn't involved in this shit is he? Like, he's supposed to be on vacation in Florida with his wife and kids. He left a week ago, though."

"Are you sure about the house?" asked John.

"Yeah, dude. I had to go by there one night when Aljie locked his keys in his car. He called me and we used my slim jim to get the door open and… oh shit!" he said, ending in a near whisper to himself.

"Okay, Joey. You've been a big help, so I'll forget about the slim jim for now…" said John, sliding the photos back in their folder. "Just don't let me catch you with it or you'll be answering a lot more questions." He smiled at Joey who was turning red from embarrassment.

John stood and held out his hand for Joey to shake. "Thanks again, Joey," he motioned two fingers at his eyes and then to Joey. "I'll be watching for ya."

As John left the bar, the scenario came together in his head. Todd had left the bar with Rachel and took her to his place. The jealous fiancée came by the bar looking for him and figured out that Todd had left with another woman.

She followed them to Todd's place, confronted Rachel about the situation, and evidently Rachel had gone commando on her ass. Todd must have freaked because maybe he happened to see his fiancée murdered in his own house. So Rachel killed him to keep him from talking. Talk about some shit, to die like that, a big guy at the hands of a woman no less.

It sent shivers up John's spine to think about it. Right at that moment, he was glad he didn't have a girlfriend. He resolved to use deadly force on Rachel if she even blinked or moved toward him when he found her. The last thing he wanted was to die at the hands of some superwoman, psycho-bitch.

Twenty

Walt was giving his next wish some serious thought while he cleaned up the fragments of Rachel's head from his kitchen floor. He was surprised that there was no blood. In fact, he used a whiskbroom and a dustpan to sweep up the pieces, and there wasn't a speck of blood anywhere when he was done.

He didn't stop to question the right and wrong of what had happened any more. Truth be told, he didn't feel much about it all. Walt stopped to ponder that fact for a moment, but soon went back to the task at hand.

The small pieces of her shattered head were no more than the size of a walnut. He didn't want to just throw them in the trash, so he emptied the dustpan into the sink each time he swept a little more.

When Walt had gotten nearly all the debris off the floor, he walked over to the sink and ran the faucet. Flipping the switch above the counter, he turned on the garbage disposal. He pushed the larger pieces into the drain and hesitated a moment when he saw one of those beautiful green eyes, now dried up and lifeless among the chunks. Then he looked away and pushed that in too.

Walt heard the crunching of the blades as the job was finished. As he switched off the disposal, he realized that the bone fragments had been so brittle that they had easily been ground up.

Next, he picked up the rest of her corpse. It weighed very little, and he put it over his shoulder and carried it down the steps to the shop below. He opened the door and walked over to where he had put Greg's remains.

He sat her next to Greg, saying, "Hey buddy, gotta girl here for ya. No struggle, no bullshit, she's all yours!" He looked at the semi-hollow eye sockets in Greg's shriveled head and said, "She isn't all that right now, but you would have liked it about an hour ago. I'll leave you two alone to get acquainted. But, Greg, forget about getting some head from this one. She's a bit lacking in that department!"

With that, Walt began to laugh hysterically. He turned off the light and closed the door behind him before climbing up the stairs to his apartment. He was still chuckling to himself when he got back to the kitchen.

"Have you decided what your reward shall be?" asked the box.

"Ooh yeah," Walt replied, "I was thinking about it while I was cleaning up your mess. You know, if you hadn't been in such a hurry to suck the spirit out of that girl, I might have actually gotten laid."

He tried to think out exactly what he would say next. After that debacle with the treasure, he needed to be more precise about his request.

"I believe I would like to be irresistible to women, that they would do anything I ask, and want me so much they might even fight over me. *That* is what I desire." He cracked a big smile and pushed his chest out like he was proud of himself for thinking of something so awesome and so foolproof.

"You are sure of this, Walt? I do not want you to be unhappy as you were with the treasures I brought to you."

"Yeah, I've been thinking about it, and I'm sure."

The box began to glow for a few seconds then stopped. Other than a slight warm feeling, Walt noticed no difference.

"That's it? So now women will want me? Is there anything special I have to do to make this work?"

"No, Walt, nothing at all. You will be desired by women as you have requested."

"Awesome," said Walt. "I want to try this out. I think I'll go out and get some more beer, so I don't have to spend any money at the Mainline later. Then all I have to do is go to the bar, order a glass of Coke, and decide who I'm gonna have sex with. We go to her place and…."

"Walt, I only need two more adult spirits. Why not bring your women here? You can do what you want with them, and then you can let me have their spirits. We can come into our time of triumph that much sooner."

"No fuckin' way!" said Walt with a sound of defiance in his voice. "I don't want you taking their spirits before I get what I want from them. You know, like you did with Rachel? No sir, I'm gonna get laid tonight, and *you* will just have to wait until later."

"If this is how you choose to proceed, Walt, we will delay our conquest until you have satisfied your carnal urges. The sooner we acquire two more spirits, the sooner you will rule by my side. You will then be able to choose from among the females of the entire world."

"Well, that is just what I wished for, right? So I can wait a couple of days," Walt replied sarcastically. "If that's ok with you, I mean? Besides, this whole 'let me have their spirits' thing is creeping me out… I never felt like killing anyone in my entire life, and now I've done it *twice* at your request and with your help. It makes me feel like shit, even when it was Greg. I mean, I know he got me fired and he really was a prick, but damn, these are real people we are killing, just so you can be reborn."

"You do not realize what power you shall wield, Walt, because I cannot share it with you while I am in this present form. When I am released from this clay vessel, you will know and feel true power. You will understand why we have done what we have done. Be patient and you will see."

"Well, like you said, I don't know what it's like. I just know that killing people like this is making me feel a little crazy.

For now, I think I'll just go to the store and get some beer. That way, I can try out my new power and let you know what I think about it."

Walt grabbed his jacket off the chair and headed out the door and down the stairs. He was whistling a song he remembered about a guy who was a *real* ladies man. He thought about what it might be like to have real sex with a woman, sex he wouldn't have to pay for. It would be a first for him. He just never seemed to have a way with women.

As he turned the corner leading to the grocery store, he could see there was something like twenty cars in the parking lot. Walking through the door, he grabbed one of the small hand baskets and headed in the direction of the beer aisle. About three aisles over, an old woman turned her head toward him, but he was oblivious to her. He was on a mission.

Walt passed the frozen foods next to the beer and wine aisle. When he came to the large beer display, he stood for a few minutes trying to decide what kind he wanted. Just then, a woman pushing a cart turned the corner. He could see her out of the corner of his eye as she stopped a few feet away from him.

The older woman, maybe in her late sixties, was wearing one of those nylon warm up outfits that seemed to be popular among her generation. She stood there looking at him and he at her until suddenly she twitched as if a chill had gone through her entire body. She took one of her hands off of the cart handle and slid it provocatively down her side to reach between her thighs. She had a half smile as she rubbed herself and licked her lips, staring directly at him.

Walt stood motionless, watching her curious behavior. She slinked toward him, unzipping the jacket of her warm up suit as she moved, exposing her plain white bra. He was so focused on her that he didn't notice the activity behind him.

Two other women had turned into the beer aisle. Apparently, they were shopping together since they had been deep in conversation. But now, the conversation had come to an abrupt halt, and Walt saw them each touching themselves in a sexually provocative manner.

Now he turned to see the older woman about two feet from him and still approaching. In his peripheral vision, there was a sudden blur as one of the other women ran past him and slammed into the old woman with a thud, throwing her into the open beer cooler display.

"Stay the fuck away from him, bitch! He's mine!" she screamed. The twelve-packs of beer that had been stacked in the cooler crashed to the floor around them, bottles breaking and the foaming beer began to spread across the floor.

"I saw him first, you bitch!" yelled the older woman, sprawled there on the wet floor. She was hurt, but still determined. As she pulled herself up, she reached behind her and grabbed a six-pack and slammed it into the other woman's head with unnatural strength. The cardboard carton ripped open, bottles smashing to the floor. The other woman reeled, letting out a howl as she slipped and fell onto the wet floor.

Walt was backing up to stay out of the fray. He couldn't tear his eyes away from the brawl. Were they really fighting over him? The two women were rolling on the floor together. He just stood there and watched, fascinated, as clothes were torn, hair was pulled, and faces were scratched. He didn't realize the third woman was moving into position behind him until she slipped her hand between his legs.

Walt's eyes bugged out as she grabbed his balls through his jeans and moaned, "You gotta fuck me! Do it right here, here on the floor."

The pain of having his balls crushed spread into his stomach, and he felt his knees beginning to buckle. He turned and jumped forward quickly to knock her loose. She fell to the floor at his feet as she slipped into the pool of beer. She began pulling off her pants, trying to get them over her laced up shoes. She was having no luck at all, but it didn't dissuade her from trying. Finally she stopped and ripped at her lace panties, exposing an ample bush of dark pubic hair.

All this had happened in a matter of moments, and Walt was beginning to realize that his wish had come true in a way he couldn't handle. The women seemed to find him irresistible just as he'd requested. They wanted him so badly, in fact, that they were having a slugfest over him.

The older woman was pushing herself up out of the beer display and the other, a younger woman, moved with her, trying to block her from getting within a foot of Walt.

Now there was movement and shouting coming from the front of the store. One of the employees, a young boy stocking shelves in another aisle, had heard the crashing bottles and was coming to see what was going on. He turned the corner in time to see the woman on the floor, who by this time was completely exposed. She was grabbing Walt by the ankle and clawing at his thighs. The boy froze there, coming on to such a sight, like when you drive by an accident on the freeway.

He tumbled to the floor as he was hit from behind by one of the girls from the checkout registers. She was running toward Walt, and without hesitation, she ran right up the poor guy's back as he rolled to a stop in front of her.

Walt dodged as the girl tried to latch on to him and she tripped over the woman on the floor, who had managed to tear off her panties, but was still tangled up in her pants.

Walt saw his opportunity and took it. He went running down the aisle toward the front of the store, dodging as he ran past the crowd of people who were waiting in line for their checkout girl to return. Through a closed checkout line, he ran out the front door free and clear.

In the line next to the one Walt had run through, there happened to be three other women and a couple of men.

The first woman was still emptying her cart onto the checkout conveyor along with her boyfriend or husband. She did not see Walt running past, but the other two women broke out of the line and came after him at a full sprint.

He was running past the glass at the front of the store. He turned his head to look back and saw the two new pursuers running behind him. The older woman from the beer aisle and her younger rival, both a bit beaten and bloodied, were limping along bringing up the rear.

The full essence of Walt's allure now had spread throughout the store, and every other woman who had been shopping there was trying to jam through the eight-woman pileup at the automatic door.

He ran about a half block and cut through an alley, gaining distance on the women behind him. When he was about 30 feet ahead, he realized that he could no longer hear footsteps chasing him, so he stopped running and looked back.

The women were standing together on the sidewalk looking at each other with that "what just happened?" look. When the older woman realized she was bleeding, she began crying and turned to limp back.

Three of the younger women, also out of their trancelike state, moved to see if they could help the older woman. Their men had just caught up to them. Walt couldn't make out what they were saying, but it looked something like, "What the hell was that about?" or something along those lines.

When he saw the men turning to look toward him, he started running again. He decided to go home and try to figure all this out. Things hadn't gone exactly as he had hoped.

Walt ducked down alley after alley, hiding behind dumpsters and poles like some Saturday morning cartoon character. Thoughts were running through his head about what had just happened, how it went down, and he wondered if or how he could control it to his advantage.

Unfortunately, he still didn't have his beer and he sorely needed something to chill out with after this. Walt decided there was no way he was going home without it. He decided to stop at a liquor store on his way home. It was owned by an older Chinese couple and should still be open, despite the other boarded up businesses in the area. Walt figured it was safe to go there at this time of day.

He moved carefully now, trying to stay in the shadows so no one would see him and start chasing him again. He covered the couple of blocks to the liquor store and stood across the street trying to see through the windows to make sure there weren't any women inside.

When he was satisfied that the coast was clear, he crossed the street and hurried through the door, the bell on it ringing as it closed behind him. He walked over to the beer cooler and opened the glass door and grabbed a cold twelve pack of Sam Adams from the shelf. As he turned to head to the counter, the beer cooler door closed behind him with a thunk.

Then he heard it.

The bell on the door made a tinkling sound as someone came into the store. Walt ducked behind a stack of vodka cases on display nearby, and carefully peeked around the corner to see who it was.

An older man came in and walked right over to a display of gin, grabbed one, twisted off the cap and chugged it straight from the bottle. The haggard man let out a belch, and Walt thought he could smell the homelessness wafting through the store.

The storeowner yelled, "Hey what you doing? You not drink, you pay! I call police!" He came from behind his counter with an aluminum baseball bat in his hand. "You stop, get out of store!" he shrieked as he smacked the homeless guy on the shoulder with the baseball bat.

"Come on, I just wanted a taste," complained the bum as he threw his arm up to protect himself.

The shop owner's elderly wife was drawn from the back room by the commotion. At first, she began to speak to the homeless man, "Hey, what you do? You…"

Then she caught sight of Walt peering around the corner of the display where he had been hiding. "OOOH…" she shuddered, "Mr. Sexy… [adding something in Chinese that Walt could not understand]. You come here Mr. Sexy!"

She started swinging her hips as she walked toward Walt. It was the exaggerated way women move when they want a man's attention. As she closed in on him, she began to moan and massage her sagging breasts with her hands. Her husband turned to look at her and yelled something in Chinese pointing back to the door she had come out from.

That was all it took to spur the passion she could recall from her youth. She ran toward Walt, tearing off her blouse as she stumbled past her husband who held the bat down to try to stop her, or maybe to trip her. There was a dull thud as she ran into the bat and went tumbling into a display of Canadian whiskey.

"Stupid woman, I tell you get back, you no listen!" He bent over her as she lay moaning on the floor.

Walt headed for the door, yelling back, "I'll leave the money on the counter for this beer!" He tossed a twenty-dollar bill on the counter on his way out the door.

The old man shook his fist and yelled after him, "You no come back! You no come back!"

Twenty-one

It took Walt fifteen minutes to walk the two blocks to his apartment and he was thirsty as hell, so as he climbed the stairs, he cracked open one of the beers from the twelve-pack. He took a long drink before he unlocked the door. Walking over to the table, he set the open twelve-pack on the table next to the box.

He sat there in silence for about ten minutes and finished the beer, then grabbed another one out of the carton and twisted the top off. As he started to drink, the box spoke to him.

"So now you are irresistible to women and they will do anything to be with you. Are you pleased with your decision?"

"Fuck you! You made all this crazy shit happen, didn't you?"

"Should I surmise that you are not pleased? You made your request very clear and direct. Perhaps next time you would like for me to provide some guidance?"

"I can't believe what just happened. Women at the grocery store were trying to kill each other to get to me! And the old man at the liquor store tripped his wife with a baseball bat! Shit, I can't even walk down the street!"

"Would you have me revoke this request?"

"Hell, yes! I can't walk around with women tearing off their clothes and beating the shit out of each other. I'll get my ass arrested, or worse, one of those old women might actually get a hold of me and… it makes me want to throw up just thinking about it!"

"Consider it done. You will not experience such things again. But, we still have work to do. I need two more spirits and then I can be reborn. I, no, We are so close. I have waited hundreds of years for this, and you have waited all of your life to have those things you desire. If you help me with this, you will no longer need to ask of what you desire, for you will have the power to manifest it for yourself. You will share the powers I possess, and you will rule with me over this world for eternity."

"Oh great. So I can fuck everything up on my own then. I can't wait!" Walt downed the rest of his beer. "What the hell? Why do things keep fucking up?"

"You will make mistakes, but you will also learn not to make them. Such great power is not without consequence, but as you wield it, there will be little to regret. You will do well."

"Well, huh? Right now, I just know I feel like shit!"

"These feelings will pass, Walt, but now we must move quickly. There is a man at the establishment where you eat, where you met with the red-haired woman. He is a lonely man, he drinks more than you, he grieves for his lost love and he wishes to die because of his pain. You will help him, Walt. You will bring him to me."

"I just got here! I don't feel like going anywhere right now. Besides, how do I know that the same shit isn't going to happen again? I don't want to have to deal with that! Take a break for a minute, huh?"

Walt looked at the clock on the wall and realized he had been gone a lot longer than it seemed and the day was slipping away.

"I understand, Walt, but to be safe, for now, we need those who will not be missed. This man will not be so easily attained again, so you must act now. He will be eager to share his sorrow with you and to come here for drink, to share his thoughts with you. So this will be an easy task."

"So we need two more? What if there are two people at the diner? Why can't I bring them both?"

"No, Walt, do not attempt to bring anyone else. Only bring the one whose wife has left him. We will find the other spirit tomorrow. You will know who, and what to do when the time comes. Perhaps you should go now before you get too, as you say, 'buzzed' on beers."

"Oh, alright! I think I know the man you're talkin' about anyway. Let me finish one more beer and I'll go." Walt reached for a beer and then sat back. "Uh, no, maybe I should just go before I get too buzzed on beers," he added sarcastically.

"Before you go, you must remove the top from this box. Then all will be prepared for your return."

"Sure, want me to scratch your back too?" Walt shook his head in amusement. He pointed his finger in the air, "Uh, wait a minute… you don't have a back, do you?" He was still chuckling to himself as he headed out the door.

Walt reached the diner in about fifteen minutes walking about as slow as he could manage. After all, he wasn't too thrilled about killing someone right now, not after all the shit at the grocery store. But now, he was there and it was show time.

As he walked in, he saw Big T in the back cleaning up as usual. He recognized the man sitting in the booth with his face in his hands. It was the same sad man he'd seen there before. Walt walked over and sat down across from him.

"Hey buddy, are you ok? Looks like you could use somebody to talk to." At that, the man looked up, his eyes bloodshot and his face red from the pressure of resting in his hands, the outlines of his fingers were imprinted on his forehead.

"Who are you?" the man rasped.

"My name's Walt. I've seen you here before, but I think you were kind of out of it then. You probably don't remember me," Walt said as he held out his hand.

The man shook his hand. "Jerry," was all he said.

"Anyway, Jerry, last time I was in, I was talking to T and he told me some heavy shit about your wife leaving you. He said you come in here often to hang out. I thought maybe you might like someone to talk to."

"Fuck, can't a man get any privacy anymore?" The man's voice was getting louder. "Why not just get a police megaphone and shout it from the rooftop, T? Hey everybody, Jerry's wife left his ass because he couldn't make her happy anymore! Besides, what the fuck is that anyway? Happy? It's all bullshit."

Walt leaned back in his seat. "Look Jerry, I feel your pain, man. I had a girl too, and she left me without even saying a word. One minute she was there sitting at the table, and the next she was gone!" He was leaving out the spirit sucking part, of course.

"Really? You mean she didn't even say anything, just left?"

"That's about it."

"Man, that sucks, but hey at least mine gave me a bunch of shit about why she was leaving before she went... gave me a chance to yell at the bitch one last time. From the sounds of it, you didn't even get a chance to do that?"

"No, it really sucked. Hey man, it looked like T was cleaning the grill when I got here, and there is no way in hell I am going to ask him to fire it up for me now. I need a beer more than a burger anyway. I have an idea. I only live a couple of blocks from here, and I just picked up a twelve pack about an hour ago. I was gonna go out later, so I can grab some fast food then. Why don't you come on over to my place and throw back a couple of cold ones with me, then we'll head over to the Mainline and see if we can't pick up some hot bitches, huh?"

"Nah, I gave up on women for now, but the beers sound like just the thing. I'm up for that. I got a buzz goin' right now, but I got no problem with taking it to the next level."

"Cool. I'm sure T wouldn't mind if you just left the money on the table. How much do you think you owe?"

"Ten bucks would cover it if I had cash, but I'm using the card tonight."

"I have a ten in my pocket, we'll just leave that and you can buy me a couple of drinks later. T hates to be interrupted when he's cleaning up. He can be quite the moody one sometimes."

"Well, hey, at least he lets me hang out here when I'm fucked up so he's not all bad. He keeps me out of jail, I guess."

Walt pulled a wrinkled up ten-dollar bill out of his pocket and tossed it on the table, then stood up and said, "Let's do this."

Twenty-two

Across town, John sat at his desk looking at his notes. He needed to find this Rachel woman and it had to be tonight. There was a lot of pressure from the media about this case, and there was a push in the department to make something happen.

He picked up a dart from his desk and threw it over his shoulder toward the dartboard behind him. He smiled when he turned and saw the dart embedded directly in the bull's-eye. This was a good omen, an indication that he was gonna get lucky tonight. He was going to find Rachel and nail her to the proverbial wall.

John stood up and put on his jacket, a vision flashing in his head of the crime scene: the woman on the floor, a headless torso and the man, Todd, with the knife thrust through his chin. Taking the jacket back off, he hung it on his chair. He took his gun from his holster and popped the clip out to make sure it was loaded. He opened the drawer of his desk and grabbed two more loaded magazines, slipping them into his pocket. Now he lifted his bulletproof vest off the coat rack and put it on. Finally, he put his jacket back on and adjusted it.

"Sometimes it pays to be like a fuckin' Boy Scout, prepared for anything," he muttered under his breath as he switched the light off on his desk. He picked up his keys and headed for the door.

~~~~~~~~~~

Actually, it was his military background that gave him the instincts to be prepared for any situation. After two years of college, he had enlisted in the Marines and found himself playing the role of a military policeman. It wasn't exactly what he had in mind when he joined up. He was more inclined to use his education to work his way up as an officer candidate.

However, during boot camp, someone noticed not only his ability to kick ass, but also his way of getting others to cooperate even when they were feeling less than friendly towards the others in the platoon.

It turned out to be something he was really good at and he developed a passion for it. He was deployed to Iraq where he eventually found himself breaking up fights between frustrated soldiers and irritated contractors. John Hazard, peacemaker... odd, but true.

He remembered putting in for a transfer the week before an ambush forced him into an early exit from the military. It was late at night when mortar shells took out three of the buildings near the mess hall. John had responded quickly. As he approached the destroyed buildings, he saw a couple of men lying on the ground, one of them on fire.

He leapt into action putting out the fire without realizing he was stepping into a trap. One of the Iraqi civilian contractors had coordinated the mortar attack with several ex-Republican Guard soldiers, and as John scooped handfuls of sand onto the burning man, the contractor came from behind and thrust a ten-inch blade through John's shoulder.

As he twisted his head to see the handle of the knife sticking up from his uniform, John spun around throwing the attacker to the ground with the force of his own body weight. He pulled the blade from the top of his shoulder, and dispatched his attacker with his own bloody knife.

Unfortunately, it was the wound that would end his military career. He was awarded a Purple Heart and a medal for saving his fellow soldiers, then honorably discharged and sent home.

After several operations and eighteen months of physical therapy, he was finally able to use the arm near its previous capacity. It took a few months of rest and self-reflection before he applied to the police academy, graduated with honors, took night classes, and made detective his second year on the force.

~~~~~~~~~~~

John knew exactly where to find Rachel's house on Maple Street. He got into his car and took the portable radio off the seat and clipped it to his belt, fastening the microphone to his shirt. He wasn't sure if he would have to call for backup or not, and it really sucked when you needed it and the radio was in the car. He turned the key, put the car in gear and headed out of the station parking lot.

He liked listening to music when he was on his way to bust somebody. He turned on the radio, and the local rock station was blasting a song called, "Better Off Dead," so he cranked it up. There was nothing better than good old heavy metal to get the blood pumping. It was the best when you were getting ready to kick in a door, and John was ready for a fight if that was what it would take to get this bitch off the streets.

By the time the song was finished, he was almost there. Right onto Lexington, left on Downing, then right again on Maple Street. Before he got to the house, he turned off the headlights and rolled to a stop across the street.

The lights on the ground floor were on, but there didn't seem to be any movement in or around the house. He got out of the car and closed the door carefully to avoid making any sound that could alert Rachel. He walked across the street, quietly opened the gate on the mesh fence and slowly walked up the sidewalk to the porch.

He stepped up the two steps and approached the door. It had a large panel of glass on it and a curtain so he couldn't see in. It was possible that someone in the house might be watching for trouble, so he stepped to the side and rang the doorbell.

No answer.

He tried again.

No answer.

There were voices coming from inside, so he went around to the back to see if he could look in through a back window. As he rounded the backside of the house, John saw a large bay window and pushed his way through the thick bushes so he could get a closer look. He saw a light flickering inside and the voices were much louder.

The television was turned up pretty loud, and was likely the reason that no one inside could hear the doorbell. He pushed back through the bushes and eased along the back of the house, until he found the back door. Three steps up, there was a screen door, and behind that a wooden door. He wondered if it was locked, how strong it was, and whether he could kick it in without a battering ram.

Walking up the steps, he tested the doorknob and found it unlocked. He pulled his gun and cracked opened the door. Peering in, John couldn't see or hear anyone at all. Opening the door further, and holding his gun in front of him, he stepped into the kitchen.

The adrenalin coursed through his veins as he walked toward the room where the television was blasting. He turned as he heard a sound outside behind him and accidentally bumped into the dining table. *Damn!*

He moved faster as he got closer to the TV room and as his gun breached it, a cat ran under his feet. He tripped, falling forward, his momentum carrying him through the doorway and into the room. He heard a loud crack as his skull hit the table holding a large potted plant next to the doorway. Just before he lost consciousness, the plant fell over on top of him and he heard his pistol discharge.

Twenty-three

As he climbed the stairs to the apartment with Jerry, Walt was suddenly struck with déjà vu. Of course, he had been having considerably more visitors lately, and he had walked each of them up these same stairs. The tragedy of this was in the realization that all of these visits had ended in the same way, and then he walked them down the other stairs to dispose of them.

On the way there from the diner, Jerry had gone into detail about what had happened to him. It was about as pitiful and painful a tale as anyone could bear.

Jerry had been a very successful lawyer in New York City and had married a woman who was more beautiful than he could have ever dreamed of knowing. Everywhere they went, people would stop to smile at her, turning their gaze toward him as if to see what kind of man could be worthy of such a woman.

For several years he had worked to defend client after client, and his rate of acquittals was very high even though some were clearly guilty as charged. So good was Jerry's rate of success that one day he received a call from one of the big crime bosses from the Bronx. The scumbag had been busted for orchestrating the murder of an entire family and faced the death penalty.

The police had gathered evidence against him and could prove he'd had the family killed for revenge. The children had been tortured to death while their parents were forced to watch. Finally, the parents themselves were tormented for hours before finally and mercifully being put out of their misery.

During the course of the trial, Jerry had discovered that the defendant had killed many people, committed multiple crimes, and had even threatened the mayor and police chief and their families with the same fate when he had been arrested.

Jerry had asked the firm to remove him from the case, but one of the partners took Jerry into the board room and explained to him that the trial would be a "walk in the park" because the fix was in. What he didn't realize at that time was that the witnesses had been threatened that they were to remain silent or be killed themselves. The arresting officer had been paid off to misplace the evidence, a member of the jury was a plant for the defense, and Jerry was beginning to wonder about the judge.

He had collected quite a bit of information through a private detective while preparing the case, and none of it supported his client's innocence. After about a month of wrangling with his conscience, he turned the file full of damning evidence over to the district attorney.

This turned out to be a terrible mistake because the D.A.'s office turned it over to the judge and, since Jerry was retained to defend the gangster, it was determined that he had violated the attorney-client privilege in the way he had gone about acquiring the information. The case was declared a mistrial, the criminal went free, and Jerry was disbarred in the state of New York.

Since his bout of conscience had kept his client and the others that were under investigation in this case from going to trial, Jerry had been given an "opportunity" to leave New York in a moving truck instead of a garbage truck.

Jerry had moved his family here hoping to start over, but he was unable to get a license to practice law in this state. After a few months of trying to find work and desperation for his future, his wife left him, took their daughter, and moved back to Ohio where she still had family. It had been three months now and he still hadn't heard a word from either of them. He wasn't even sure if she had gone to Ohio because every time he called her parents home, they said they had no idea where she was.

Jerry had been living on his savings and the money was about to run out. Since he'd been drinking so much, he'd made some very bad decisions and he confided to Walt that he often considered suicide since it didn't seem like it would ever get any better.

All of that should have made things easier for Walt, take him inside and put him out of his misery. The box had told him that the people he was bringing in were those in the dregs, who had little reason to live in the first place. But Walt saw a little bit of himself in every one of them and, if he had any compassion at all, it was for people like Jerry.

As they neared the top of the stairs, he turned to Jerry and said, "Look man, maybe instead of coming inside, you should just go home and get some sleep."

"Nah," replied Jerry, "I'll sleep when I'm dead, right now..." he pulled up his sleeve, "...according to my watch, it's drinking o' clock!" He laughed heartily at that.

Walt hesitated at the top of the stairs with his hand on the doorknob. Maybe Jerry could get his life together. He was young and smart. Obviously, there were folks a lot worse off than Jerry who had pulled their lives together and made something of themselves after some great tragedy in their lives.

He was just about to tell Jerry he'd changed his mind about hanging out here when Jerry opened his mouth and spoke the words that signed his death warrant.

"What the fuck, man? You some kind of fucking weirdo or something? Invite me, bring me over to drink some beers and then stand here outside the door? Is this really your place or are you stroking me?"

Walt was stunned. This was the last thing he had expected to hear now. After all, he'd been kind enough to invite the guy over, and he'd listened to his entire sob story on the way over.

Jerry went on with his tirade, "You a homo, Walt? Was this some trick to get me over here to try and suck my dick? Having second thoughts? You fuckin' faggots are all alike!"

There was no hesitation now. Walt could do this and without any qualms. All the compassion he had mustered up for the guy was gone now, and he opened the door. "No man, I'm not a faggot, I just thought…"

"Well, don't think so much, you might pop a vein! Man, you better have at least a case of beer here, or I'm gonna have to whip your ass and send you out for more." Jerry laughed too loudly at that one.

Walt could feel his blood pressure rising and his face growing hot as he reached in and turned on the light. "After you," he said and motioned for Jerry to go inside.

As he stepped into the apartment, Jerry complained, "Dude, what's that smell?"

"Smell?"

"Yeah, smells strange, kinda like nasty dirty ass warmed up! Maybe something dead, a squirrel in the attic?"

A look of shock spread across Walt's face. Jerry was really close to the truth, but not close enough to save himself from it. Maybe the dead bodies downstairs were starting to smell. Could anyone smell it from the street? What if someone walked by and smelled it and called the police. Shit! Now what was he going to do?

Then Jerry started laughing and said, "Just kidding, Walt, where's the beers? You looked like you swallowed a cat there for a minute, dude. You all right?"

Walt felt dizzy. He looked at Jerry, forced a smile and thought, *It's Spirit Suckin' Time, you fuck!* But all he said was, "Not a cat, just for a second I felt a little sick, but it passed. How about that beer now?"

"Oh yeah!"

Walt walked over to the refrigerator to get the beer as Jerry sat down in his mother's favorite chair. He turned around and saw Jerry sitting there and said, "Hey... uh, sorry... not there. Sit at the table. I thought we could maybe play..."

"Yank my crank, faggot?" He smiled as he was saying it. Obviously, he had some issues he hadn't mentioned during the walk over and it was really starting to piss Walt off.

"Uh no," replied Walt. "I thought we could play some cards or something."

"Oh yeah, play some poker. I'll take all your money!" He got up from the chair and walked toward Walt. There was a crunching sound from under his foot as he neared the seat at the table. He lifted his foot and saw something like cookie crumbs there on the floor. Although, there among the crumbs was a painted fingernail and a cheap silver ring.

Walt stiffened. *Holy shit, was that Rachel's finger?* He kept his eyes on Jerry as he reached toward the counter where next to the sink sat a cast iron frying pan.

Jerry bent over to pick up the ring and look at it.

"You're quite a slob aren't you Walt? You should try cleaning once in a while. Hey, I have an idea. Twice a year, when the time changes, like changing the batteries in the smoke alarm, Walt cleans house!" He opened his mouth to laugh, but Walt had grabbed the skillet from the countertop and swung it in one swift movement to slam into the side of Jerry's head before the laugh could escape his lips. Instead, all that came from him was "UGHHH!" and he fell over on his side.

Quickly Walt dropped the skillet and grabbed Jerry under his armpits and lifted him to the chair and dropped him into it in front of the Spirit Box.

"Kill this fucker!" he yelled anxiously at the box.

The blue light started to rise up from the box and Walt stepped back. He reached for his beer and twisted off the top, gulped down half the bottle and watched as Jerry began to shake.

"Who's the faggot now, motherfucker?" Walt yelled as Jerry's spirit passed from his body.

Twenty-four

The smoke alarm was emitting a loud screech when John finally regained consciousness. The room was quite smoky, and he coughed and choked as he pulled himself to his knees. John reached up and rubbed his head, which hurt like hell, then sat on the floor trying to get his bearings.

Had someone hit him from behind? Was someone else here? No, he remembered tripping over the cat. Coughing again, he realized that the room was beginning to fill with smoke and got in position to crawl out of there.

About five feet away he could see the hole in the side of the old style television that he had shot as he fell. Flames were racing up the walls on two sides of the room and the fire was spreading fast. John looked around to make sure there were no signs of anyone else in the house before leaving. He couldn't see anyone through the thick smoke.

He was crawling now, pulling his shirt up over his mouth and nose to block out some of the smoke. He moved in the direction of the back door where he'd come in, since he knew it was unlocked. He opened it to exit, and before he had a chance to breathe, the fresh air whooshed in and, boom, John was blown through the open door, out onto the backyard.

He lay there dazed and in pain for a moment then reached up for the microphone of his radio. Nothing was there but a dangling cord. Was it ripped off his belt in the explosion? He reached down to his belt, and found the radio still clipped to it.

"This is Detective John Hazard. I have a 251 - house fire at 1267 Maple Street. Send an ambulance."

"Ten Four detective, units have been dispatched and are on their way. Do you require uniformed backup?"

"Uh, that would be a negative," John answered.

"Dispatch standing by."

He stood up and looked around. It appeared that none of the neighbors had even noticed the fire yet and no one seemed to hear the smoke alarms still blaring inside the house. He could see the glow of the fire on the house next door and hear the wood in the walls crackling as they burned. The alarm was suddenly silenced, and a large pop and a crash could be heard as one of the windows blew out.

"Fuck me," he said to himself. How was he going to explain this to the captain? Okay… he was following up on a lead and happened on the fire, so he called it in. He got injured when he tried to go in and see if there were any people in the house. The air rushed in when he opened the door and fed the fire, blowing him out through the door. Perfect!

It was a better story than trying to explain breaking and entering, conducting a search without a warrant, discharging his firearm and every other mistake he had made that could *maybe* cost him his badge. On top of everything else, could a murder charge be involved if there was someone still in the house?

"Shit! Fuck!" He said again as these thoughts raced in his mind.

From down the street he could hear approaching sirens, the fire trucks were getting closer. He walked around to the front of the house and waved as the trucks pulled up.

"The fire started in the back. I couldn't tell if there was anyone inside!" he yelled as the firemen jumped from the truck, began unrolling hoses, and removing the cap from the fire hydrant about twenty feet from the house.

Right about then flames hit the gas lines inside the house and the resulting explosion blew out the front windows and door along with half the front wall. Flames shot out about twenty feet from the house and the firemen ducked for cover as debris blew over their heads.

The house was now fully involved and flames were licking up the outside walls, melting the vinyl siding and adding to the voracity of the blaze. The firemen had two hoses connected. One was trained on the fire and the other on the neighboring house, trying to prevent the fire from jumping to it and taking out the neighborhood. Another truck came screaming down the street, and behind it an ambulance.

The men from the third truck connected their hoses and directed the flow of water from the burning house to the house next door. The ambulance driver walked over to John, "Hey buddy, are you all right? Looks like you got your ass kicked judging from the blood running down your face."

John had been so freaked out by what had happened that he hadn't noticed the blood from the large gash on the side of his head. When he reached up to feel for it, he pulled back a bloodied hand. Suddenly, he felt dizzy and the pain registered in his brain. The ambulance driver stepped forward and put his arm around John and helped him to the back of the ambulance. He opened the door and helped John step up and sit down at the back of the truck.

"So, what happened to you? Was there a blast?" He pulled a penlight from his pocket and flashed it in John's eyes, first one then the other.

"How are you feeling? Are you nauseated? Do you feel dizzy?"

"No and yes"

"Look, you might have a concussion. I think we should transport you to Lincoln General and have you checked out."

"No, I'll be alright. I need to stay here until they get this thing put out. I need to know if my suspect was in there when this thing went up…"

"Look, man you could be seriously injured. Are you sure you don't want it checked out?"

"I'll be fine. I just need to get back over there," said John, groaning as he got to his feet. Then he took three steps and fell to his knees and threw up on the ground in front of him.

The ambulance driver ran to his side and asked, "Look, I think we should take you to the hospital. Are you sure you are going to be OK?"

"No, I'm fine. I just need to rest here for a minute!" he yelled over his shoulder. Wiping the vomit from his chin with his hand, John continued to walk away.

"Ok then, if you're sure you're okay. Far be it for me to tell a cop what to do!"

John walked over to his car and got in. Looking in the mirror, he took a paper napkin that was lying on the floor on the passenger side and began wiping the blood from his face and the stream of vomit dripping from his nose.

It took about thirty minutes for the firemen to finally extinguish the fire. The Fire Marshall had arrived and begun a cursory inspection of the steaming ruins of the house. After about an hour of watching him work his way carefully through the charred ashes, John got out of his car and walked over to him.

"Do you think anyone was in the house? Did you find anything?"

"No, no one was inside as far as we can tell, but we have a lot of ashes to go through still."

"What do you think started it?"

"Looks like the point of origin was the back room. Coulda been the TV was the culprit. TV's, especially the old ones, are a big cause of fires. But it is the weirdest thing…"

"What did you find?" asked John, feeling his ass cheeks tightening.

"Well, the TV looked like it had a bullet hole in the side."

"If there was a gun involved," John answered, "I need to check it out for myself, take the round if I can find it to the lab for ballistics tests. This is a crime scene as far as I'm concerned."

"Well, I don't think that'll be a problem as long as you don't disturb anything else in the house until I complete my investigation."

"Oh don't worry. At this point, only that TV is of interest to me."

With that he walked around to the back of the house as the Fire Marshall shouted after him, "Hey be careful I haven't had a chance to check the integrity of the floor back there yet."

"Yeah, I'll watch my ass. Don't worry," John yelled back as he stepped through the burned doorframe.

The place was still steaming and smelled like burnt plastic. He looked through the doorway into the room where the TV had been and, even from where he stood, he could see the bullet hole in the side of the melted plastic of the shell. It was an old portable TV sitting on top of an old console TV, the consummate redneck home entertainment center.

As he walked over to pick up the portable TV, he glanced down at the floor and saw a picture frame lying beside the floor model TV. He bent over and picked it up. It was a photo of an attractive girl with red hair and some guy sitting at the ocean somewhere. The girl was striking a sexy pose, but you could get a good look at her face as she looked into the camera.

This must be the infamous Rachel. It would be a big help when asking people if they know her. John took another look at the girl in the skimpy bikini. She seemed to look right back at him and, for a moment, he lost sight of what he was here to do. Standing there in the steamy room, looking at such a beauty, he felt his blood rush. The girl was totally hot!

No, this was all wrong. He shouldn't feel like this about a cold-blooded killer. He turned the frame over and slid the back off it, then removed the photo and shoved it in his pocket. He tossed the empty frame aside and picked up the partially melted TV.

Rather than taking any more time to "examine" it, he decided to carry it outside to look for the bullet. He needed something to use to pry the cover off. As he stepped through the rubble, he looked around for a knife or a screwdriver or some kind of tool.

As he neared the back door, the floor beneath his right foot gave way. His leg went through to just below the kneecap and as he fell forward, the TV crashed to the sidewalk at the bottom of the steps. The half melted cover flew off revealing it's electrical guts.

John groaned as he pulled his foot out and pulled up his pant leg to look for signs of injury. Nothing but scratches this time, except for a large splinter in his calf. He grit his teeth as he pulled it from his calf and threw it to one side. "Damn, that fucking hurts!" he said, wiping the blood from his fingers on his shirt.

He limped down the steps and bent over the remains of the demolished TV. It was pretty burned up. He could see that the old style tube had been struck at an angle by the bullet, which had caused the bullet to slam into the circuit boards. He saw a hole in one of them, pulled it aside and there was his bullet, wedged in among the transistors.

He pulled it out and shoved it in his pocket and hobbled back toward his car shaking his head. He yelled at the Fire Marshall, "I'm done here for now, let me know what you find… especially if it's a body." With that, the detective got in his car, and drove off.

He turned at the corner and pulled over. Staring out through the windshield, he took a moment to gather his thoughts. Then he sighed. "Man, I'm too young to be too old for this shit!" He put the car in gear and drove off.

Twenty-five

Walt stood by the table looking at Jerry's shriveled corpse. He pushed it with the toe of his shoe, moving it a few inches across the floor, leaving a greasy smudge on the tile.

"See bitch, I don't suck but my box does. You should have left when you had the chance. You actually had me feeling sorry for you, there for a minute. I can see now why you lost everything, stupid bastard, don't know when to shut up!"

He paused holding his hand up to ear as if expecting a response, then continued, "I have a few friends down in the shop I think you should meet anyway. I think you and Greg will get along just fine, and maybe Rachel will let you break off a piece! Literally!" He roared with mad laughter.

Maybe he was losing his mind. Maybe he was just tired, since he couldn't remember the last time he had slept peacefully.

Jerry had tried to run when the box started ripping out his spirit. He had stood up partway and turned, so his legs were twisted up like a pretzel. Because it was impossible for the victim to look away while the box was sucking out its spirit, Jerry's head was turned back to face the box, snapping his neck during the process. Now his head flopped over to one side with his mouth grotesquely distorted.

With his spirit removed, his body had dropped gently back into the chair. Walt was thankful for that because there would be a much bigger mess to clean up had the body fallen to the floor. He walked over to open the door to the stairway leading down to the shop. He wanted to be prepared, so he went on down the steps and opened the door at the bottom.

Walt went back upstairs and reached to pick up Jerry when his phone rang.

His phone never rang. But there it was, ring, ring, ringing.

He considered letting it ring, but it didn't let up. He figured he must be about the only person in the world without an answering system, but some time ago he had decided that he don't need one if nobody ever called.

Finally, he picked it up.

"Hello?" It was a somewhat familiar woman's voice. Maybe one of Mother's old friends who didn't know that she had died.

"This is Walt. Who's calling?"

"Walt, it's Kathie from work!"

Walt felt his cheeks warm as his blood rushed. "Kathie? Hi, I didn't expect to hear from you. What's up?"

"Oh Walt, you left and didn't even say goodbye. I didn't even know they fired you until somebody in the break room told me. 'First Walt got fired, then Greg Walker disappeared'. That's what everyone's saying. Sorry I called so late, but I've been trying to get up the nerve to call... and... and I had a couple of glasses of wine... and I know it's late, but I really wanted to see how you're doing."

Walt was surprised to hear from Kathie. During brief conversations at the office, he'd often wondered if she had any interest in him, or if she was just one of those people who's friendly to everyone. Many times he'd considered asking her out, but he managed to talk himself out of it every time. So here she was calling *him* tonight.

"It's nice of you to call to find out how I'm doing. I am *definitely* missing the old job and the gang over there." He lied, looking at Jerry's body still slumped in the chair.

"I miss you being there, too," she said. "You were always so nice and polite and treated me like a girl likes to be treated, not like the other animals there. Sometimes, it feels like I'm working in a zoo!"

Ok, so how should he handle this?

"Well, it'd be great to see you sometime if you have the time. I mean, you know, just to talk and have a coffee or something. We could just hang out… I mean, if that's okay with you," he offered, biting his lip.

"That sounds really nice, Walt. I don't have anything going on tonight… I mean, if *you* aren't busy, maybe we could meet for drinks somewhere. Maybe at the Mainline or something?"

He looked over at Jerry's corpse, and thought for a minute. "Well, to be honest, I *am* kind of busy right now cleaning up a mess at my place… but would tomorrow after work be good for you? Maybe we could meet for dinner and…"

"Sure, tomorrow after work is great! Do you like the Downtown Steakhouse? They have a *great* salad bar!"

"That sounds real nice, Kathie. How about six o'clock then?"

"I'm there, Walt! I can't wait to see you again! Bye-bye for now, see you at six tomorrow!"

"Sure thing."
He hung up the phone and smiled.

Twenty-six

John went straight home feeling slightly bruised and toasted. He walked in the door and emptied his pockets, and poured himself a short glass of Gentleman Jack. At the refrigerator, he shoved the glass under the ice dispenser and click, click, click, no ice.

"Fucking piece of shit!" he muttered under his breath, opening the freezer door. He shoved his hand into the ice bin and punched the block of ice cubes to break them apart, then closed the door. When he put his glass under the switch this time, he heard ka-chink, ka-chink, as the ice was dispensed. "Now that's what I'm talking about."

He turned and walked over to the lamp table by the door where he'd emptied his pockets. He picked up the photo and the round from his gun that he'd taken from Rachel's house and sat down on his old worn out green sofa.

The remote control was on the floor in front of the sofa. He picked it up and pressed the button to turn on the TV. It was one of those expensive remote controls that had to be programmed, but once he'd figured it out, one button turned on everything, the TV, the cable, the surround sound, and even the video player, just in case. His entire entertainment system came to life.

John set the remote and the photo on the coffee table and sat there holding the bullet up to get a closer look at it. Fortunately, it had been fairly easy to find it. He set it next to the remote and picked up the photo of Rachel. Striking red hair, incredible curves, and a flawless tan.

"Wow, you are a babe…" he said out loud. She just smiled out at him. Too bad about the guy in this photo, he was really messing up the mood of the scene.

John got up from the sofa and went into the kitchen where he opened a drawer and pulled out a pad of paper and a roll of transparent tape. He tore off a piece of paper and a strip of tape and carefully taped the paper over the guy in the picture.

He smiled at his handiwork because it accomplished just what he wanted, Rachel alone in that sexy pose with no distraction from the other guy. He could understand why she was so popular down at the Mainline. She had great tits, not too big, not too small, and no scars or stretch marks, or any flaws anywhere that could be seen in the photo, anyway.

Her ass looked nice and shapely, nice well-rounded hips, not like some girls with no shape. No sir, this was the real deal and, for a redhead, Rachel had a nice tan. She wasn't one of those pale white redheads. Ahh… this was rich… this was rare… this was just what he needed after the night he'd had.

He was already getting hard, and he reached down and rubbed himself through his pants. He pulled down his zipper and eased "the Beast," as he referred to it, out. He chugged the rest of his bourbon and winced as it went down. Then he grabbed his favorite toy and began to stroke.

Twenty-seven

Walt carefully picked up Jerry's body. It was surprising how light a person could be after the box was done with them. He knew to be careful when he was lifting and moving them after what had happened earlier with Rachel's finger.

He should have known better after carrying Greg's body down the stairs when he'd accidentally bumped Greg's arm against the doorframe. It had snapped off and fallen to the floor, bits of it breaking off and scattering. It just made a bigger mess that he had to clean up.

Walt started whistling as he worked, thinking about Kathie and his date tomorrow. It was still hard to believe that she had called, and even more unbelievable that it seemed she really did miss him being at the office. Or was she just curious about his relationship with Greg? Had Greg told her about his prank? Was she trying to investigate whether he knew anything about Greg's disappearance?

As he let this thoughts go around in mind, he remembered that he now had a wish to use after this last spirit deal, and he decided he would use it tomorrow night. If he played it right, it wouldn't matter what her intent was.

After the box did its thing, he could literally have anything he wanted from her. Anything!

When he got to where Greg and Rachel were laying on the floor, he set Jerry down beside them. "Jerry, this is Greg and Rachel. They stopped by earlier and decided to stay awhile. I'm kind of thinking the three of you might get along pretty good after you spend some time getting to know one another."

Walt made sure that the bodies were set up so none of them fell over. "In fact," he went on, "I would suggest a three-way, except that I don't think Rachel can get her head around that idea right now."

He laughed. "She just fell to pieces the other night, and she just can't get it together."

He turned to walk away when he heard a woman's voice behind him say, "You think this is funny, Walt? Wait until you find out that the only joke in all of this will be the one that's being played on you!"

"What?! Who said that?" Walt looked around. No one was here except the three corpses, and they sure weren't talking. "Shit, now I'm hearing voices… and it's not even the weird Spirit Box voice… I need a drink."

"A drink won't solve your problems, Walt." The voice came from behind him again but this time from the other side. He turned and saw Rachel standing there in front of him. At least, it looked like Rachel with her head intact, but she was quite transparent and he could see right through her.

"You're not real, you're dead! Your body is right over there!" he said pointing at the corpses, his voice shaky now.

"Gentlemen, we have a winner! Yes, Walt, I am dead, and you are not seeing or hearing me right now. Since you really don't see or hear me, it's going to be hard for you to understand it when I tell you that the box is not going to share anything with you. Not the world, not the women, not the treasure. He, or it, needs a slave and playing the slave is a part you play rather well, judging from your performance so far." She winked at him and was gone.

He wasn't about to hang around and wait for anyone else to talk to him. He broke into a run, turned the corner, and ran through the door slamming it behind him. Quickly he turned the lock and ran up the steps and locked the door at the top of the steps as well.

"Something wrong, Walt?" he heard the box asking him from the table.

"Yeah," he said breathing hard, "I think I just saw Rachel down in the shop, at least it looked like her and she was talking to me. That can't be real, right?"

"Others have told me about this in the past, Walt. In fact, it was once explained to me by a scientist nearly a century ago. It is like a ripple in a pond when an object is dropped into it. The ripples are not a part of the object, but they carry a representation of the mass of the object, thereby displacing a projection of the object in another form. It is somewhat confusing, but what you have experienced is a projection of Rachel's spirit."

"Well, that scared the *shit* out of me down there!"

"I understand. Since we only need one more spirit and then the vessel, it is unlikely that you will have that experience again. Have you decided what it is you desire as your reward?"

"Yes and I've thought carefully about this. I'm meeting Kathie tomorrow evening, and I want her to like me so much that she feels that she is in love with me. That should be easy enough without any problems, right?"

"Love always comes with problems, Walt, but it should be easy enough to grant your wish. If it is not already so, so shall it be. When you meet with her, things should go very well indeed."

"They better, man. This has been a lot of hassle so far and I really don't care for killing people." Walt reached up and turned off the light above the table, looked around for anything out of place, then got ready for bed. Just as he was falling asleep his last thought was of Kathie, having dinner with her, and gazing into her eyes, eyes that would shine back at him with love.

Twenty-eight

John was lying on the sofa, exactly where he had passed out the night before, his pants still unzipped and a trail of drool tracked across the pillow where he had buried his face. He got up and went to the bathroom, looked in the mirror and turned on the faucet. He let the water warm up a bit then put the stopper in the drain and waited for it to fill up.

Shoving his face into the full sink, he came up shaking his head. With both hands he splashed more water over his face. Then he grabbed a towel from the rack and wiped the dripping water from his chin. He picked up a throwaway razor from the counter and dragged it over his face, shaving without any shaving cream or soap. With a dull razor, it was as though he was ripping the hairs out with his bare hands.

John had shaved this way lately. He didn't get as close a shave as when using the cream, but it gave him a great look around three in the afternoon, kind of like one of those detectives from that television show in the eighties. The ones who wore the fancy suits, drove the fast cars, and best of all, had sex every episode.

He dropped his pants and stepped out of them, snagging a washrag off the towel rack, he shoved it in the water, ringing it out and gave his package a quick scrub. He grabbed some clean underwear out of the laundry basket and pulled them on. John finished dressing, pulling some of his clothes from the basket, some from the hamper, and then he was out the door without so much as a cup of coffee.

On his way to the station, he stopped by Big T's Diner and grabbed a cup of free coffee. Free coffee and donuts for cops at Big T's made it one of the most protected businesses in town.

He arrived at the office at about 9:15 and found a note stuck to his monitor that read, "See me now! Chief." He ripped the note off and headed down the hall to the chief's office. As he got to the office, one of the patrol officers was leaving and he didn't look too happy.

"It must be ass chewing day today..." he joked as he knocked stepping through the door. The officer stopped and glared at him, then turned and walked away. John heard him say a muffled "asshole" as he left.

"It's my destiny to be the leader of fools and assholes," said the chief, "the fools make me laugh and the assholes bring me nothing but trouble, so which are you today, John?"

"Uh, a detective sir? Unless you take stock in what Jenkins said as he was walking away, then I guess I would be the latter."

"Exactly Hazard, you are a detective – a damn good one, and that is why I summoned you here! We got two separate missing persons reports last night, one for a woman named Rachel and one for some guy named Greg. I want you to handle both of these cases."

"What was the woman's last name?"

"Keane. Rachel Keane. Why?"

"Lives over on Maple Street, or I should say lived, her house burned down last night. The Fire Marshall said that it could have been her television that started the fire. Who reported her missing?"

"We got a call about 5:15 last night from her mother, who lives somewhere in Kansas, I believe. She said she hasn't heard from her daughter for about a week, and that's unusual because this Rachel calls her every three days like clockwork. What do you know about this woman, detective?"

"Well, Chief, I've been investigating that double homicide, and she's my only suspect at this point... what about this Greg guy? What's the story on him?"

"He's been missing from work for a couple of days without calling in and some of his co-workers reported it. Here's his address, I need you to swing by there this morning and check out his place. If you have to, kick in the door on suspicion of a crime being committed and see what you can find. My guess, he's on a drinking binge, probably ashamed of himself, or he might be dead, who the hell knows what you might find." He shoved a case folder into John's hand and turned toward the window. "Dismissed," he grumbled over his shoulder.

As John walked out of the office, his mind was on Rachel. He had spent the night with her, the beauty in the photo. "Damn shame," he said as he sat back down at his desk.

Twenty-nine

Walt spent the morning cleaning the apartment. He was hoping that he and Kathie would have a great time and she would really like him. If the box didn't screw up his wish this time, he figured they might need a place to go after dinner.

He got down on his hands and knees and looked around the floor for any signs of body parts that may have broken off any of his latest visitors. If Jerry had seen the finger on the floor before he stepped on it, things may not have gone so well. He wanted to be extra careful to get every bit of trash and clutter that might have gotten knocked loose or kicked under some furniture.

The box had been quiet all morning. Walt guessed it must have been planning for ruling the world or something, an idea that Walt found to be more than a little humorous. He guessed he was having his chain yanked, but he had seen that the box could really produce the goods when it came to fulfilling his desires. Even though every time so far the whole thing got fucked up, there was still some serious power behind it.

Besides, who was he to stand in the way of the next *King of the Whole Fucking World?*

Kathie took her seat in the boardroom at 9:15 sharp just like she did for all the morning meetings, which began at 9:30. She carried her notepad and two fresh pens from the supply closet. She had a bit of OCD when it came to taking notes.

Everyone else filed into the room five or ten minutes later and, when Mr. Palmer finally arrived, he had another man with him. This guy looked like he had dressed himself from the clothes hamper, his shirt and pants were badly wrinkled. Not a very snappy dresser, that was obvious. The door was closed and the meeting began.

"Thank you all for coming this morning," Palmer began. "The reason for this meeting, as some of you may already know, is that Greg Walker has recently been reported missing. Since it appears someone here was the one to report it, we have been asked by Detective Hazard here to provide any information that could help him locate Mr. Walker. Mr. Hazard? Go ahead." Mr. Palmer stepped back and remained standing, leaning against the wall with his arms folded.

John stood up, leaning on the table. He nodded toward Mr. Palmer. "Thank you, sir. Look I don't want to take a lot of your time this morning. I just want to introduce myself and ask if anyone working in this office might know anything that may be useful in this case. Some of you may know something, and some of you may not know that you know something. Then again, some of you may not know anything at all that can be of help. So I am going to remain here, right in this room after this meeting for about a half hour. If you think of anything at all that could be of help, please take a few moments to meet with me before I leave.

"If any of you have any knowledge of someone who might have had a reason to be angry with Greg, or whether he had a gambling or drug problem, that is the kind of thing that could be helpful. He might have had an ex-wife or girlfriend that he was having trouble with. Mainly we are looking for anyone who might have known Greg Walker outside of the office."

At that point, John scanned the faces in the room looking for signs of someone who might be fidgeting or appear to be uncomfortable. Some of them had been nodding while he had been talking. There were a few smirks and bits of laughter as John spoke, so he assumed that someone here might know something.

He pulled a stack of business cards from his pocket and handed them to the woman who was sitting closest to him. "I'm going to hand out my business card. Like I said, I will be here for about thirty minutes. After I leave, if you think of something, no matter how trivial you may think it to be, please call me at the number on the card. That's my phone at the office, so leave a message for me if I'm not at my desk. I will get back to you as soon as possible. That's all I have for now, so thank you all, and thank you again, Mr. Palmer." With that, John sat down.

"You're welcome, Detective," said Mr. Palmer, stepping forward. "If anyone knows anything, please take a few minutes to talk to the detective. Greg was a good employee here and we want to help in any way we can."

As each one received John's card, they stood and went back to their desks. All but three people, two men and one woman remained seated. As the others were shuffling out of the room, John said, "I am assuming that you three might know something, so let's take this one at a time. First, I'd like your names." He reached into his jacket and pulled out a flip pad and a pen. "Ok, you first," he nodded to the dark-haired woman across the table.

"Carol Altin."

"Thanks, Carol. Now, if you don't mind, I'd like you to return to your desk for a few minutes and I will have someone call you when I'm ready to take your statement."

Carol got up and walked out, turning to wave to the younger of the two men left behind.

"Ok, and you sir?" John motioned to the balding man with wire-framed glasses.

"Bill, Bill Haxwell,"

"Great, Bill would you mind waiting at your desk also? When I'm finished with…." He pointed with his pen at the second man sitting at the table.

"Tony. My name's Tony Polimo." Tony sat back against the chair with his arms folded. He appeared to have an athletic build.

"When I am finished with Mr. Polimo here, I'll have him let you know that I'm ready for you. Cool?"

"Yeah, Ok…" Bill said as he left the room.

John followed him to the door and closed it. Then he walked back to the table and sat in the chair across from Tony.

"So Tony, you think you might know something that can be of help?"

Tony nodded.

"Would you mind if I record your statement?"

Tony shook his head, indicating that he didn't mind.

"Great," John reached into his jacket and pulled out his small pocket recorder, pushed the button on the side, sat it on the table between them and began to speak. "This is a statement from Tony, is that Anthony?" He looked at Tony.

"Yeah"

"This is a statement from Anthony Polimo regarding the Greg Walker missing person case. Okay, Mr. Polimo, go ahead tell me what you know about Mr. Walker."

John was aware that when you call someone Mister, rather than by his first name, the formality would get a better result than being on a first name basis. He guessed it was a respect thing. By showing the witness respect, the witness would be more inclined to be forthcoming.

On the other hand, this guy could be a suspect trying to hide his involvement in the disappearance. If that were the case, calling him Mister would make him uncomfortable and help to reveal that he might be hiding something. John wondered if it was the cat and mouse games that he loved about his job or was it just that he despised scumbags?

"Ok, well, you know you said something about gambling and drugs and stuff? Well, Greg has been doing some of that stuff lately and he might have gotten in some trouble."

"Go on."

"Well, he'd bet quite a bit on a football game about a month ago, and I know he was having some trouble paying off the debt after he lost."

"And how do you know about this debt, Mr. Polimo?"

"Well, he made the same bet with me on that game. When I asked him to pay up, he told me he couldn't because he'd lost a bundle and he didn't know how he was gonna pay a debt to me when he had lost so much to his bookie. He was strapped for cash."

"Do you know the name of this bookie?"

"No, I just know he said something about a bookie and he wanted me to go in on it with him, but I was sure that team would lose so I made a side bet with him myself and he refused to pay when he lost."

"How much are we talking about here?"

"Well, with the odds and everything he owed me about two hundred bucks."

"And were you angry about this, Mr. Polimo?"

"Yeah, he said he had the cash at home when he made the bet." Then his face went red. "Uh, I didn't do anything though. You think I killed him and put him in the trunk of a car or something like that?"

"Slow down, Mr. Polimo. Should we take a look in your trunk then?" John asked smiling.

"No, he isn't in my trunk. I swear I didn't do anything to him. I just thought you should know about the other thing. He said the guy would have his legs broken or something if he couldn't come up with the cash!" Tony was looking frustrated and scared as hell.

"Okay, okay. I'm just messing with you. Cool down. We don't' have a crime yet as far as I know. We're just trying to figure out where to look for Mr. Walker. Do you know anyone who might know who he made the bet with, or can you tell me how much he bet with this mystery bookie?"

"About two thousand, I think."

"Name?"

"No, like I said, he never mentioned it."

"Okay then, I'll let you return to your desk and if you think of anything else, you'll call me, right?"

"Sure will," Tony was breathing easier now. "So that's all you need me for?"

"Yes, would you please send in Mr. Haxwell?"

Thirty

Walt was changing the sheets on the bed when the box finally spoke again.

"Walt will you be sleeping in your bed tonight instead of out here on the furniture? I am sure you will rest much better in there."

Walking to the kitchen, Walt replied, "Did you say something?"

"I asked if you were preparing your bed for the night? Will you be alone in your room tonight, or do you have plans to bring that woman here and take her into your bed?"

Walt felt his face warming with rage. "I might bring her here and you will not bother to speak to her if I do! Do you understand?"

"Of course, Walt. I would not think of scaring this woman away. You did wish for her affections, did you not? I am aware of your feelings for her, how deep they burn within you. You wish to copulate with her, as all men do with the women they desire, which is why you have prepared the bed for her. Is this not so?"

"That's right, so don't fuck this up for me!"

Walt turned and went into the bedroom to finish cleaning. He wanted everything to be extra nice for what he hoped would be a special evening the next night.

The next afternoon, Walt was still feeling anxious about his meeting with Kathie. No, not so much anxiety as a feeling of exhilaration and anticipation. This was a groundbreaking moment in his life, this attempt to establish a real relationship with a woman that could go beyond friendship.

It was time for Walt to be on his way, but first he needed to find a way to get downtown since he didn't have a car of his own. It would have been nice if he could have recommended a decent restaurant within walking distance for their meeting, but there was no such thing.

He went to the end table next to the sofa and reached down to pick up the phonebook that had been stashed down there forever. Taking it from the shelf, he blew the dust off and opened it. He looked up taxi services, picked up the phone, and called the Limited Cab Company for a pickup. The taxi arrived no more than ten minutes later and he was on his way.

Meanwhile, Kathie was just getting off work. Before she left, she went past the cubicles where Walt and Greg used to sit. There something caught her eye. It was a post-it note pad on the desktop and on the top note was scribbled "Walt 6PM." Greg was not known for legible handwriting, so it kind of looked like it said, "Malt 6DM." She stared at it for a minute, but it was clear that it was Walt, not Malt.

She tore the small square of yellow paper off the pad and put it in the pocket of her form fitting, stretch tan slacks, and then moved around the cubicle wall to where Walt used to sit. Since he'd been fired, Walt's computer and monitor had been removed from the desk, and there were only a few loose papers scattered about.

Kathie sat down in his chair and spun around a couple of times. Out of curiosity, she opened the drawer to the left of her just to see what might be left there. There was a small cardboard box that appeared to have been used by Walt as an improvised desk organizer. In it were a plastic saltshaker, some ketchup packets, a few pens, two permanent markers, some napkins, and about two dollars in change.

As she was retrieving the change from the drawer, the napkins moved to the side and she saw a small strip of leather with a buckle on it. She pulled it out from its hiding place and then realized it was not just a leather strip but a woman's watch with a leather band, one of the old wind up ones.

She decided she would take it with her, but rather than carrying it in her pocket, she fastened it around her wrist. It was a nice old watch and in pretty decent shape. She wondered if it still worked. She took hold of the stem and wound it a couple of times, then held it up to her ear. It was ticking in a quiet steady way, and the second hand was moving, so she pulled the stem out again and set the time to the clock on the office wall, 5:15.

Kathie was running late, and Walt might get upset if she kept him waiting for too long. She remembered her mother used to say, "Never be on time when it comes to men, they might expect that from you every time, and being late adds a bit of mystery. You just don't want to seem too anxious by being on time."

Maybe Mother was right because now she really was feeling anxious. She had been looking forward to this dinner, dare she say date, all day. She put everything back in place in the drawer and closed it. She stood up, straightened her clothes and headed for the door.

She went out into the parking lot and got into her ten-year-old, green BMW and turned the key. It wasn't much to look at after all these years, but at least it was reliable and started on the first try. She put the shifter in "D" and tooled out of the parking lot and into the street, heading for downtown.

Walt's taxi pulled up to the restaurant at five o'clock on the dot. He half expected Kathie to be waiting for him out in front, but then he remembered that she usually left work around 4:50, so he wandered in to ask if there was going to be a wait.

Inside there were only about ten people in the dining room, five of them seated at one table in the corner. At another table, it appeared that the manager was finishing up some paperwork and was having a conversation with one of the waitresses. They were laughing about something and, as they turned to Walt, the waitress's face grew red. She stood up suddenly and hurried back into the kitchen, disappearing behind a swinging door.

He walked over to where the hostess was fumbling with the menus and some coloring placemats and stated, "I don't need a table yet, I'm waiting for someone – she should be here soon."

"Yeah? OK."

It felt good to announce that he was waiting for someone. Walt had never had such an opportunity to do that before, at least not with a date. He'd been out before with his mother, but not with a girl he really liked, and who seemed to like him too.

There were some benches near the entrance, so he sat down and tried to read the cards and look at the photos that had been posted on the bulletin board on the opposite side of the short hallway. He guessed that the photos were those of patrons, and as he scanned them, his eyes fell upon a picture of a beautiful red-haired woman with some man. He stood up and moved closer to get a better look. It was a picture of Rachel, and she was with Greg!

Suddenly he was overwhelmed with a mix of feelings, remorse, guilt, fear and dread. Here he was, waiting for the one girl he might have a chance with and across from him was a photo of two people he had assisted in murdering! To make matters worse, the dried husks of their bodies were now sitting in the dark of the shop below the very apartment where he hoped to take Kathie later.

In a moment of panic, he reached over and pulled the pushpin from the corkboard and took the photo and shoved it into his pocket. Then he sat back down with an expression on his face that could only be described as the cat that was just caught eating the family bird.

As he looked around to see if anyone was watching, the hostess called to him, "Are you okay sir? Do you need a glass of water or something while you wait?"

"No! Thanks, but my friend should be here any minute."

Just then Walt saw someone outside. The door opened and Kathie stepped inside, taking a few seconds to allow her eyes to adjust to the dim light of the room. Walt stood to greet her, and suddenly Kathie turned as a big smile formed across her face.

"Walt!" She stepped forward and threw her arms around him, hugging him and pressing up against him. In a low voice she said next to his ear, "I really missed you, Walt, but until now I didn't know just how much." Then she kissed him on his cheek, startling him. He felt embarrassed and tried to pull away.

"Uh, Kathie," his face blushed, "hi, I missed you too."

"Oh, Walt, there is so *much* to talk about. Let's get a cozy booth," she said as they walked toward the hostess station. The hostess looked up from her seating chart and asked, "Will that be two for dinner then?"

Walt nodded and the hostess pulled two menus from the side of the station. "Right this way."

"Could we have a booth please? Something private would be good," asked Kathie as she pressed close to Walt, still clinging to his arm.

The hostess walked them to a booth near a window and placed the menus on the table. "Phillip will be serving you tonight, and he will be right with you." She removed two of the place settings from the table and walked away.

"Oh Walt, it feels like it has been forever since I've seen you. How long has it been exactly?"

"About a week or so I guess."

"I feel so full right now Walt, not in a just-ate-dinner kind of way, but like… well, I guess like it might feel to be in love or something. I just don't understand it, I've never felt like this before…"

"I know what you mean!" Walt was having feelings too, only he was feeling like he was being watched or something. Like someone in the room knew what he had been up to for the past week and at any moment they would walk over and expose him and his evil deeds.

Instead, the waiter came over and asked them if they would like to start with drinks. Walt asked Kathie what she wanted. "You order for me. Surprise me, Walt."

He ordered two draught beers and an order of potato skins with sour cream and bacon. He could sense Kathie staring intently at him. "What's the matter?" he asked.

"Walt, I don't want to freak you out or anything, but I just have to tell you… I really love you, and I don't know if I can stand to be apart from you ever again. I know it's kind of sudden, but I feel like I'm going to die if I don't have you inside of me!"

Walt stared at her, with a look of astonishment that was bound to be obvious. He hesitated, and said, "Well, I think maybe we should eat first. I'm kind of hungry, and I haven't eaten anything all day. After that, we can go to my place if you want?"

When they were seated, he thought Kathie had sat across from him so they could look at each other while they were talking. Now he realized there was something more to it, as he felt something moving against his leg under the table. He leaned over to see what was going on to see that Kathie had taken off one of her shoes and was rubbing her foot against him.

She pushed her foot up inside his pant leg. She was grinning as she pulled her foot back out and began vigorously running her foot up and down his leg to his crotch. Then she made contact.

Walt wasn't at all prepared for her to be acting this way, certainly not in a restaurant. She had aroused him to the point of erection, and he was quite embarrassed since nothing like this had ever happened to him before. Worse than that, up until right now, right here, he had never imagined that it ever could.

"Walt, can I move over there and sit next to you?" She asked in a deep voice, almost begging.

He started to agree, then realized that she may have ideas of going further than she had already done. It was highly likely since now she was methodically rubbing his erection with her foot and grinning like the Cheshire Cat.

"Are you ready to order?"

The waiter's question startled Walt, and he jumped visibly as their drinks and appetizer were placed on the table.

"Do you need a few more minutes?"

Walt panicked… could the waiter see Kathie's foot planted in his crotch? Were they going to get thrown out for being obscene? What the *fuck* was going on?

He asked Kathie, "Do you know what you want?"

"I want you, Walt. I want to eat your…"

Walt cut her off, "We'll have two T-bone steaks with fries and a salad!" He said quickly, "Blue cheese dressing, Thanks!"

Kathie started giggling as the waiter turned and walked away. "I want to eat you up, Walt. Oh, I want you so bad!"

"Sure, okay, we'll get to that," he grabbed his beer and took a long drink from it, finishing almost half of it. As he reached for a potato skin, Kathie leaned over in the booth, slid under the table, and she was gone. He felt her maneuvering around the post that supported the table and he leaned back and looked down into her eyes.

"Hey, uh Kathie, I think we should wait until after dinner, then we'll go to my place and I'll let you do anything you want. Deal?"

She looked up at him like a sad puppy and hesitantly said, "Okay, deal." Then she backed up and climbed back into her seat.

"Hey Walt, can I sit next to you?"

Again she was smiling at him, all teeth and gushing.

"Not right now, let's just cool down for a minute before we get arrested," he said and picked up another potato skin and steered it toward her pouting lips.

She grabbed his wrist, the food just inches from her lips. "Arrested? I can't help it, I have never felt like this before. I want MEAT, Walt!" she hissed.

"I just ordered you a steak! Just hang on for a few more minutes."

"No, you don't understand baby. I need *man* meat, *your* meat!" She moaned. Childlike, she started chanting, "Walt Meat! Walt Meat! Walt Meat!"

Walt looked around. Until now, no one had seemed to notice the woman in heat sitting across from him, but now he could see another woman at a table across the room lean forward, look at the man across from her, and whisper something. Then she looked toward Walt with a disgusted expression on her face. When she noticed Walt looking back at her, she faked a smile before she took a bite from her very large salad.

Thirty-one

Detective Hazard sat at his desk looking at the three photos of the missing people that were growing into a grim collection of faces, characterizing a situation that was very unusual for this small town. Rarely did anyone ever go missing in this county and, even when they did, they usually showed up in a day or two.

John stared at his monitor. A little bit of research into several data resources showed no activity on financial accounts of any of the three. There were no call records on their mobiles recently and, for the most part, it had been family members who had reported them missing.

So what was the common denominator between these three people, if in fact there was one? Rachel had apparently just met her victim, Todd. Jerry had recently moved to the area from New York City, and Greg was just a womanizing nobody working at a small local company. Although, from the interviews with company employees, it did seem that he could possibly have some enemies, or at least some people who might be upset with him.

John sat back and crossed his arms behind his head and closed his eyes, letting his mind relax, hoping that something might come to him. A half hour later, he woke up with drool running down his chin, and he finally came to the conclusion that there was no common link.

There was only one thing to do. He'd take the photos to small businesses, public places in the area and ask folks if they had seen these people together at any time in the past. If he could establish a common thread between them, he might be able to connect the dots, find the missing link, and solve this strange puzzle.

He gathered up the papers and photos from his desk and returned them to the folder, then shut down his computer and turned off the light on his desk. Tomorrow was going to be a very long day and he was not looking forward to it.

Thirty-two

Kathie choked down her steak dinner so quickly that Walt thought he might need to use the Heimlich maneuver on her. He had never seen anyone eat so fast, not even the guys he had lunch with. At one point, he had a vision of one of those wood chippers that chews up a tree branch so fast that you could lose your arm if you lost your concentration. He could almost hear the chipper as she hammered through another bite.

As she was eating, she continued rubbing her foot up and down his leg. Like an animal rubbing itself against him, the movement of her foot was steady and persistent. All the while she maintained eye contact and occasionally winked at him between bites.

Suddenly she finished eating and sat staring at him. She did not stop rubbing his leg, which was now beginning to feel carpet burned. She licked her lips and said in a low tone, "I'm ready for dessert, Walt, and I'm thinking of an éclair with lots of creamy filling!"

He could swear that all of the hair on his leg must have been rubbed off by now. He gulped, "You are?"

"Oh, yes, and as soon as you are finished I think we should go to your place and have some of that, that good stuff," she gushed, winking at him. "Hurry up and finish that now, baby. I'm on fire and I need the fire hose! Waiter!" she called out loudly enough to turn all the heads in the restaurant. "Check, Please!"

Phillip walked over to the table with the black plastic folder containing the bill, "Will there be some dessert tonight?"

"That's what I'm talking about!" sighed Kathie, "Most certainly, and here is my card. Please hurry back. Run!" She handed him her credit card in the black folder.

"So you do want dessert? I'll go get the tray so..."

"No I wasn't talking about that! No dessert, please. Go take care of the check so we can get out of here."

"Certainly."

As Philip walked away, Walt finished off his potato and swallowed the last of his beer. "I guess you're ready then..." He dabbed his mouth and wiped his fingers on his napkin.

She was standing at the end of the table reaching for his hand. "Let's go baby."

"What about your card?"

She looked at him in exasperation, and strode across the room where Phillip was processing the credit card. She snatched the card from his hand, signed the receipt, spun on her heels and almost ran back to Walt. She put her arm around him and pushed the keys into his hand, "I want you to drive, honey, so I can feel you on the way to your place."

Walt hesitated to take the keys from her hand, "I think maybe you should drive, Kathie. I've had a few beers, and I wouldn't want to damage your car with a fender bender." In reality, it had been years since Walt had driven a car, so he wasn't sure he was ready to jump behind the wheel the way he was feeling right now.

She pouted, "I'll drive if you insist, but you have to tell me where we are going. I want the fast way, not the route that takes us past the park, mister!" She shook her finger in his face.

"Sure, no problem. Where's your car?"

"Follow me!" She pulled him toward her car showing a strength that seemed more than normal for a woman of her size. When they got to the car, there was a parking ticket on the windshield. Ignoring it, she got in and leaned over to unlock the passenger door while at the same time turned the key in the ignition.

"Damn parking tickets," she said, turning on the windshield wipers and rolling down the window. As the wiper swished toward her, she grabbed the ticket to free it from the wiper blade and let it go, leaving it to flutter in the tailwind of the car as she sped up and drove down the street. "Which way, honey?"

"Turn left at the next light." Walt said, as he clicked the latch of the seatbelt into place. He was amazed at how this evening was progressing. He never could have imagined such a wild ride, both figuratively and literally.

A series of turns and fifteen minutes later, Kathie pulled up in front of the shop and turned off the engine. Walt had counted five stop signs, and three red lights she had run on the way there. Then there was the guy in the crosswalk. He looked familiar for some reason, but it was hard to tell for sure from the way he was screaming as Kathie just barely missed him.

Walt wasted no time in getting out of the car and moved around to Kathie's side to open the door for her as she got out. "It is so cool that you live above the antique shop!" she said, "I'll bet it was really interesting to grow up meeting all of the people who used to shop here."

"I wouldn't exactly call it interesting, but it was unusual. I can't even imagine what it would be like to live in a normal family, in a normal house. I've been here all my life."

"Well, honey, I'm just glad you have a place to go. Let's get upstairs. I've got something I want to show you." She grabbed Walt's hand and dragged him to the stairwell.

They climbed the stairs together and Walt unlocked the door, stepping aside as he opened it for her. He followed her in and closed the door.

"So where's the bedroom then?" she said, already unbuttoning her blouse.

Walt stared at her as she threw her blouse to the floor and stood wide-eyed as she unhooked her bra and let her shapely breasts break free. Walt's jaw dropped as he took in the sight, a sight he had never seen before up close and personal.

"You are as beautiful as I'd always imagined you might be," he said. "I can't believe you're here with me."

"Believe it," she took his hand, "this will be the night we tell our children about."

"Children?!?" replied Walt, stunned.

Thirty-three

John woke early in the morning, feeling pretty decent for a change. In fact, he decided he might just go out for breakfast, maybe head on down to the diner and have some real food. He hurried and shaved, showered and got dressed. He grabbed up all of his pocket stuff: wallet, keys, change, and fastened his shoulder holster in place as he put on his jacket.

He walked to his car whistling to himself and, as he climbed into the driver's seat, noticed the file folder still on the passenger seat where he'd left it the night before. He decided he might as well take it with him to breakfast so he could prepare for questioning employees of the businesses in the area.

He started the car, pulled out of the driveway and drove to the diner, listening to some classic rock on his car radio. After a few minutes he found himself singing along, lost in a song from his childhood, and before he knew it, he'd arrived at the diner.

He parked his car close to the door and walked inside, "Mornin', T!" he shouted at the big guy through the window to the kitchen.

"Hey, Detective! Good to see ya. You want the usual this morning?"

"Sure thing. Need coffee right away. I'll help myself, since I can see you're busy." John walked around the counter to grab a coffee cup and filled it to the top. As he set it on the counter, it spilled a bit over the lip of the cup onto the counter. He walked around the counter and took a seat on the stool facing the fresh cup of coffee. Then he reached over to take a napkin from the holder and wiped up the coffee spill.

He had carried the folder in from the car and he opened it now, taking the photos and spreading them on the counter. He sat there staring at them a while. In a few minutes, T came from the kitchen carrying a plate full of eggs, hash browns, bacon and toast and set it on the counter to the side of the photos.

"Working on a case, John?" he asked filling a small glass with orange juice.

"Yeah, we've got two murders and three missing people right now, and one of the missing is my murder suspect. It's the damndest thing. I can't figure out what these people might have in common, if anything."

"Some crazy shit for a small town, eh? Keepin' you busy?" T stood holding the pitcher of orange juice and looking down at the photos.

"Crazy shit is right. Take a good look at the photos, T, and see if you recognize any of them."

"Sure," he said, setting the juice on the counter. John turned the photos so T could see them better.

"Oh shit, John!" he said, "I've seen all of these people in the past week or so, right here in the diner!"

John perked up, "You have? Were they in a group, or by themselves? It would be really weird if they all went missing together, wouldn't it? Like something from a movie."

"Well, they were here alone at first, these two, and this one came in for lunch a couple of days ago." T was tapping the photos with his finger as he spoke.

"What do you mean by these two were alone at first... then what?"

"Then I saw Walt sitting with them and they left here together. Just kinda slipped out the door and left money on the table. I didn't think anything of it really."

"So some guy named Walt came in and these two left with him. All of them together?"

"No, I mean it was different days, but I'm sure these two each left with Walt on different days. The other guy just came in by himself and then left alone, I think, but I can't be sure. You know I get busy here sometimes."

"So who is this Walt your talking about?"

"Walt is a regular. His mother used to own the antique shop down the street, but she's dead now and he comes in a lot. He used to come in on his lunch break when he worked for that computer company, but I think he lost his job, got fired or something like that.

"Come to think of it, he hasn't been here at the usual times lately, and the last time he was here he didn't seem as talkative as usual. Actually, the last couple of times he didn't talk much at all to me. Just slipped in and left with these folks."

"Do you know the name of the computer company where he used to work, T?"

"I think it was something like, Obelisk. Yeah that's it. Obelisk."

John wondered if T could hear the puzzle pieces click into place in his head. Obelisk is where he'd interviewed Greg's co-workers, and now it seemed like this Walt guy worked there too. To top it off and make all the pieces fall into place, Walt had been fired!

Talk about a lucky break! Now he'd need to make another trip to Obelisk to research the connection between Walt and Greg. If there was a connection, and John supposed there was, maybe he could somehow connect the other missing persons too.

"Hey T, excuse me for a sec. I need to make a call."

"Sure thing," said T. He went to work cleaning up some dishes and wiping up something spilled on the counter.

John took out his phone and the business card from Obelisk that was in his pocket and began to dial.

Thirty-four

Walt was tired, emotionally and sexually worn out. He couldn't remember ever feeling so drained or so satisfied. Of course, he'd had sex before, like the first time in high school. But, back then, he was so inexperienced and so was she, and even though it seemed awesome at the time, it was nothing compared to this.

Besides, Mother had interrupted that time and he was so traumatized by that experience, he didn't remember that part. She had told him about it several years later. She used to throw that guilt at him a lot when she was feeling sorry for herself.

"Walt, I can't believe you would do that to your mother," she would say, "after what I saw you and that girl doing, and her father saw it too. You are so lucky I was there or he would have thrashed you to within an inch of your life."

She would go on and on, "But no, I stood up for my boy, no matter what, and when I need you now, where are you? Sitting around in the apartment while I'm breaking my back in the shop to support you?" That tactic always worked to keep him in line. How could he argue with someone who saved his life and sacrificed everything for him?

Later, after he became more desperate for some female company and a little release, there were the hookers. They had lots of experience, but it was hard to relax and enjoy the experience when, every other breath they took, they were telling him to "Hurry up and give it to me, baby," so they could move on to the next customer.

But tonight, here was Kathie. She really did make love to him, and for so long. He had no idea how many times she had been able to make him hard again. He only knew that his mind was reeling from so much pleasure over the past several hours. He was now exhausted, and sore all over, as he lay on the bed. This really was what it felt like to be in love. Wasn't it?

Kathie had fallen asleep with her last words ringing in his ears. "I don't think I've ever done that before, especially that many times. I wanted you so bad..." No one had ever told him they wanted him "so bad," and he had never wanted anything so bad either. What would it be like to have this with her for the rest of his life? He just knew she was the one he had been waiting for.

Sure, he had loved Mother, but that kind of love felt much different than this. In fact, compared to the overwhelming love he felt for the woman he'd spent these last hours with, any other kind of love was really kind of hollow.

"We're downstairs wondering what you're going to tell Kathie when the cops come and take you away?" came the voice from beside the bed. He was so startled that he almost fell to the floor, and nearly woke Kathie from her exhausted sleep.

It was Greg, or at least something that looked like Greg, but it flickered in and out. "You are gonna pay for this, shithead. You can't get away with what you've done to us. People are looking for us, and for you, and there's no way to hide it for much longer. They are closer than you think..."

"Get out of here and leave us alone!" Walt whispered as loudly as he dared. "I don't need this crap from you right now! You'll wake Kathie."

"Even if she did wake up, she can't see me. I am here for you alone, and it's you who should get out while you still can. You are *so* screwed, and I don't mean like what you and Kathie just did. I see something like total hell for you in your future, like ripping flesh and screaming agony." He grabbed at his head as if in pain and his hands passed right through it.

"Do you really believe that the thing in the box wants to be your friend, Walt? Don't you think that line about 'ruling the world' is a load of crap? As soon as you give it the last thing it needs, it will rip you apart. You're nothing to it."

"Get out, Greg! Like I should believe you, the guy who fucked up my computer, then sits back and laughs when I get fired. Sure, Greg, I saw you. I saw all of it and I really don't care what you think about any of this any more. I have everything I need now, and I definitely don't need friends like you!"

"You're already dead, Walt. You just don't know it yet. You just don't know..." Greg said, and faded away.

"Did you say something, honey?" Kathie said quietly from beside him.

"No, it was just a dream. Go back to sleep." He tried to reassure her. She made a muffled sound and started snoring. He rolled over on his side and wondered how much of what Greg said was true, and what was bullshit. A panic began to weave its way through his brain. Like icy fingers around his neck, he was aware of his throat tightening. His chest felt heavy and the sweat was breaking on his forehead and running down his cheek.

Greg was right about one thing. With the bodies downstairs, he was so fucked. Sooner or later someone would piece together that he was the last person to see Greg alive, and then the cops would come. He just needed to be ready when they did.

He decided to put a plan together tomorrow after Kathie had gone home. Everything would be cool. He just needed to keep his shit together. Yeah, everything was going to be all right. With that he drifted off to sleep.

Thirty-five

The sun was just beginning to rise when Kathie opened her eyes. She looked over at Walt still snoring and smiled thinking that she had never felt so exhausted and physically sore from so much sex. She had been a wild woman last night. She had done things to him that she had only fantasized about doing before, and it actually felt good to finally get it all out of her system.

Carefully, she slipped out of bed and looked around the room for something to wear. Walt's bathrobe was draped over a small chair in the corner, so she slipped it on and went into the bathroom. She closed the door and looked around. *You can tell a lot about a person from their bathroom,* she thought as she stood in front of the mirror.

This bathroom was extremely clean for a guy who lived here alone, she thought as she opened the medicine cabinet to see what she might find in there. Pain reliever, toothpaste, razor, and shaving cream. Nothing too unusual. Nothing to be concerned about, so she closed the cabinet door and looked at her hair in the mirror. She grabbed a hairbrush from the back of the toilet and quickly brushed her hair. *Good, that's better.* She wanted to look good for Walt when he woke up. Maybe she should fix her makeup? No, it would be okay for right now.

She decided to sneak out to the kitchen and make some coffee, maybe even some bacon, eggs and toast. Then she could surprise Walt with breakfast in bed. Didn't all men love being served? Why should he be any different? She opened the bathroom door slowly to avoid making any noise and tiptoed out of the room, heading for the kitchen.

It was a nice tidy little kitchen, with plaid curtains on the window over the sink and red tile on the wall above the counter and below the cabinets. A small nightlight to the left of the sink gave her the light she needed to do some minor things without turning on another light.

Looking at the layout of the cabinets, she chose the one that she thought might contain coffee and she was right on the money. Coffee and filters sitting right where she had figured they might be.

Kathie took the supplies from the shelf and pulled the coffee maker out from under the cabinet so she could fill the water reservoir. The pot was clean and empty, so she filled it with water and poured it into the top of the coffee maker. She added the coffee and pushed it back under the cabinet to wait for it to finish brewing.

She went to the refrigerator and pulled the handle. The door made a loud squeak as it opened, and she cringed and looked toward the bedroom, straining to see if the sound had awakened Walt. No, he was still snoring like a chainsaw.

Inside the refrigerator was the usual bachelor fare: mustard, ketchup, beer, more beer, and a bag with moldy bread in it. "How can guys live like this?" she whispered to herself, closing the door. There wasn't even any milk for her coffee!

As she turned to find a place to sit down and wait, she noticed something glowing on the kitchen table. She couldn't make out exactly what it was, but it seemed to be some kind of a lamp glowing a bluish color. She hadn't noticed it earlier. She looked for a light switch and turned on the lamp that hung over the table.

"What an unusual piece of pottery," she marveled as she looked at the box on the table. The lid looked just like a crown and was off and laying beside it. She sat down to get a better look at the face that was carved into the side of it.

It was quite beautiful and the face was so realistic that each individual hair on the beard was distinguishable from another. She could see now that the blue glow was coming from inside of the box, and it was getting brighter. She grasped the box and tilted it toward her, peering inside to see where the light was coming from.

She wasn't sure what she was seeing there, so she looked a little closer. Suddenly, she realized what it was and exclaimed, "Oh my God! Is that a human heart?!"

In the other room, Walt opened his eyes and stretched. He hadn't slept that good in such a long time. He could have sworn that he heard a door closing earlier, but right now he was still a bit groggy so he wasn't sure. He lay there and looked around, relaxed and basking in the memories of the night before, and then it hit him.

"Oh shit, where is she?" he said out loud. He jumped from the bed and ran into the bathroom where the light was still on, but she wasn't there. He turned and ran for the bedroom door and he could see a pale blue light coming through the doorway. Then came the bloodcurdling scream.

"Kathie NOOOOOOOOOOOOOOOO!" he yelled as he ran for the kitchen. As he passed through the doorway he looked toward the table. Kathie was standing with her mouth open so far that her lower jaw touched her chest. Her spirit was halfway out of her body and it was looking at him as if begging him to help her.

As he watched in horror, he could see her skin shrivel before his eyes. Her spirit flew into the box and her body began to fall to the floor. Walt was running toward her, reaching forward to catch her. As he came to a sudden halt, the momentum caused him to fall forward on top of her desiccated body. With a crackling sound, her body broke into pieces and he landed on the pile of her broken body parts. Dust and particles flew everywhere.

For a moment he lay there stunned, tears flowing from his eyes. Then the anger overwhelmed him and he pulled himself up to face the box.

"What the fuck did you do to Kathie?!?" he yelled, shaking both fists in the air. "Why did you kill her, you fucking maniac? I love her! She was my chance at a real life!"

Silence permeated the room, with nothing but a fine mist settling around the now closed box. Walt stepped forward and grabbed the box trying to pull the lid off, but it would not budge. He was sobbing uncontrollably now, his anger and grief overcoming him. He turned with the box in both hands and threw it against the wall.

It hit with a thud, punching a triangular shaped hole in the drywall, and fell to the floor. Again he tried to smash it, this time throwing it on the tile floor of the kitchen. Instead of shattering, it bounced, cracking the floor tile where it hit.

Walt was enraged. He went to the closet in the kitchen and retrieved his claw hammer, laid the box on the floor and began pounding on it. The noise was nearly deafening as the sparks flew with each stroke. Not only did the box appear to be unbreakable, there was not one mark on it anywhere.

Trembling, Walt picked the box up from the floor and shook it. "What the fuck are you made of? I want to destroy you, you motherfucker?!" he screamed. He walked toward the door, unlocked and opened it.

Holding the box in front of him, he stepped out to the landing, leaned over the rail and threw the box to the ground below with all of his might. The box struck the pavement, bounced and rolled a couple of feet away, coming to a rest on its side. It lay there for a moment, and then flipped itself upright.

Walt stood for a moment looking at it before he ran down the stairs and walked over and picked it up. He looked at it in the morning light. There was not a mark on it, not a scratch. It actually reflected the light and rays were dancing off the building as he turned it.

Tucking the box under his arm, he climbed the steps to his apartment, went inside and set the box on the coffee table by the sofa. He turned and looked at the pile of broken body parts that used to be Kathie on the floor, and he leaned forward with his head in his hands and began to sob again.

Thirty-six

At 8:45, John was sitting in his car in the parking lot at Obelisk. He saw the office manager pull up so he got out of his car, crossing the parking lot to meet her halfway to the door.

"Excuse me," he called to her as he caught up. "I'm Detective John Hazard. I was here the other day to interview some of your employees and ..."

"Yes, detective, I remember you."

"Right, well anyway, I need to talk to your HR manager for a few minutes to get some information on one of your employees, or maybe I should say former employees, if that would be all right."

"Oh sure, she should be here any minute. You can wait inside if you like."

"Thanks, that would be great," he replied and followed her as she unlocked the glass door and walked in. First, she turned off the alarm at the entryway and then flipped the switches that turned on the lights in the offices. John found a sofa to the right of the door and took a seat.

After about ten minutes, a blond-haired woman walked in, straightening her windblown hair. As she walked past the reception desk, the office manager called out to her, "Sherry, this detective is waiting for you. He needs to talk to you about one of the employees."

Sherry stopped and looked at John, then held out her hand as he stood. "I'm Sherry Glennen, and you are…"

John held out his hand and shook hers. "Detective John Hazard. Miss, uh, may I call you Sherry? I was wondering if I might talk to you for a few minutes in your office, privately."

"Of course, detective, uh, John. Right this way."

As they walked down the hall to her office, Sherry started asking questions, "So tell me, detective, you want to talk about one of our employees? You look kind of serious about this, did something bad happen?"

"Well, that depends on what you mean by bad," he said as they stepped through the doorway of the office, and she closed the door behind them.

"I guess if you consider murder or persons reported as missing bad, then yes, it's bad."

"Oh my, and one of our people has something to do with all of this?"

"Possibly. I need some information about an employee named Walt. I don't have the last name, but I think he may have been recently fired or laid off."

"Oh, Walt. Yes, he was recently fired. Let me get his file for you. Oh, I should ask… do you have a warrant?"

"Warrant?"

"A warrant to access the information. We can't legally provide personal information about employees without a warrant, at least I don't think we can."

"You don't need a warrant to give me his last name and address."

"Is that all you need, then?"

"Yes, I just need his full name and address. I don't care about his work history. I just need to know where to find him. I would really like to ask him a few questions."

"In that case, I don't think that would be a problem." She said, turning on her computer, "I just need to wait for my screen to come up so I can access the information."

"No problem, I understand."

"So, while we're waiting, is Walt missing or involved in a murder?"

"I don't know yet, but one of your other employees has been reported missing. I have heard that Walt sat next to the guy who's missing and was seen with him in the diner down the street a few days ago, right before the guy was reported missing."

"Big T's Diner?"

"Yeah, you've been there before?"

"Yeah, I had lunch there just yesterday. Wow, you just never know, do you? Okay, it's up now, Walt's last name is Turner."

"Address?"

"Four Twenty Seven, East Elm. I think he still lives above that antique shop on Elm. I gather from what I've overheard from office conversations that Walt is kind of a strange character. Keeps to himself a lot."

"I'm not surprised to hear that. Thank you so much for your help. That's all I need right now. I'll be in touch if I need anything else. You've been of great service to your community, ma'am."

"No problem. Have a nice day, detective."

Thirty-seven

It was close to 11:30 in the morning, and Walt was still sitting on the sofa staring at the coffee table. He knew that he needed to get himself together and do something with Kathie's remains, but his anger and anguish were paralyzing, and he found it impossible to function.

Somehow, even in his current state, Walt had managed to place the box back on the dining table where it had been before, and the thing had been silent all this time. His attempts to destroy it had failed completely, and the only thing to do now was to wait for it to speak to him once more and confront it with his questions. He needed to know why it had done such a thing to the only woman who had ever told him she loved him.

He stood up from the sofa and crossed the room to the dining table, stepping over the pile of dry body parts that was once his new love, Kathie. Walt slumped into the chair where Kathie had last sat.

"So are you going to tell me why you did this to Kathie, when I asked you specifically not to take her? You said that you understood, then you killed her, you sonuvabitch!"

"I did not do it, Walt. It was you."

"Me? Motherfucker! I saw you take her! I didn't do anything. This wasn't supposed to happen! This isn't the way it was supposed to go..."

"You should not have brought her here, and not have let her near me. You ignored the truth, Walt, the reality that I only needed one more spirit. You ignored the facts, and now she is indeed gone."

"You didn't have to kill her! No one made you do it!"

"But I did have to do it. This vessel demands it. It is the price I have paid for hundreds of years. The price to live, yet again. You see, Walt, none of this is how we would like it to be, and sometimes there is no choice. In fact, it was her destiny to be my final spirit. You will understand that soon enough."

"So you knew you were going to do this, and you just didn't tell me? You've known about all of this ahead of time, haven't you? I will find a way to destroy you. There has to be a way."

"Ah, but it was also your destiny, Walt. In the new world that we shall create, there is no place for this woman, this object of your affection. She would have made you weak and unable to fulfill your life's purpose.

"It is a delusion to believe that the woman held you in her heart on a daily quest for your love. Before you asked to be the focus of her affection she was afraid of you, and her conversations with you were an attempt to allay those fears. She tried to face her demon, and ultimately her demon brought her here to her own end."

"How should I know if what you say is true, that she was afraid of me? Maybe that's what you want me to believe so I won't work harder at trying to destroy you."

"I am confident that you know in your heart that her love for you was not true. Over time, the spell on her would have come to an end. She would be the woman she was before, the woman who paid little

attention other than forced, friendly greetings to you as you worked with her for those many years."

"Oh, fuck you! You don't know shit! I am sick of you and your 'rule the world' bullshit! I can't take any more of this killing. I'm up to my ass in dried-up prune corpses, and you keep asking for more! Sooner or later someone is going to kick in my door and haul my ass off to jail. You won't be getting any more spirits when I'm strapped into the electric chair!"

"There is only one more task for you to complete, Walt, and then you will see that what you have been told is true. After I am reborn, no one will ever try to lay a hand on you without permission. Would the servant dare to kick in the door of the palace, when surely he would be torn apart and fed to dogs? Your power will be such."

Walt stared at the box shaking his head in silence. He felt he would explode at any moment. What was this damn box talking about? Did it not understand that he had been pushed beyond the limit of what he could take with all of the killing and the promises?

"I told you I can't take any more of this shit... if you need another spirit, just fucking take mine! I don't have a job, nobody gives a shit about me. I don't need to hang around here any longer. Just fucking kill me too!"

"Is that what you desire, Walt? I am obligated to provide you with what you desire after bringing the woman to me."

"Yes, suck the spirit out of my body and turn me into a dried up pile of shit like you have done to everyone else!" Walt's tears were streaming down his face now, and he was bracing himself against the tabletop, waiting for the process to begin. He closed his eyes and opened his mouth.

"Come on! Just fucking do it! What are you waiting for? I don't have all day." Again Walt closed his eyes and opened his mouth wide waiting for the life to be sucked out of him.

"Walt, I can not remove your spirit. You see, to do so would require me to remove your soul as well, and that is just not possible."

"Not possible? Because you already have what you need to be reborn?"

"It is true that I have reached the full number of spirits I was bidden to collect. Now the only thing I need is the newborn infant child. With that…"

Walt's eyes popped open, "A baby? You never said anything about a fucking *baby*! Shit! What do you think; I can just go to the store and steal one from a shopping cart or something? This is insane! Come on, take my spirit and my soul!"

He expected to see the blue light, but nothing happened. "What are you waiting for? This is bullshit! Why don't you kill me? You don't seem to have a problem killing anyone else."

"Walt, you do not understand. I cannot take your spirit and your soul. You do not possess these human characteristics."

"What are you talking about? I'm right here living every second of this crap. Are you are telling me I'm already dead? Am I a fuckin' zombie or something?"

"Not dead, Walt. It is not about living or not living. You see, Walt, you have no spirit and no soul because you were never born of a human parent."

Walt started laughing hysterically. Now he knew the *Great Spirit Box* was full of shit. He turned and walked toward the door and stepped out onto the landing. He was beginning to feel dizzy so he sat down on the top step and put his head down, resting on his hands.

This could just *not* be true. He had just lost the only woman who had ever shown interest in him, besides his mother, and now he was being told by some antique piece of pottery that he had never been born. Or was the box implying that his parents were aliens? If that were true, it would explain why he didn't feel like he fit in when he was with other people.

Am I seriously considering the possibility?? Walt sat for a few minutes thinking about the entire state of affairs. Suddenly, he stood up and walked back into the apartment.

"So, Mr. Box, you seem to know everything about me. If I was never born, how did I get here?"

"Do you wish to know everything?" asked the box.

"What the hell do *you* think? Yes, everything!"

The box began to tell him his story.

"Your mother was a lonely woman. For many years she suffered, trapped in a loveless marriage to a cruel man. Finally, she came to understand that she was living with a husband who had no desire for a normal life or a family. Each time she expressed the desire for children, he threatened to leave or he physically beat her.

"After nearly twenty years, she had given up hope that she would ever enjoy the experience of raising her own child. In an attempt to free herself of the darkness overtaking her soul, she began to plan a trip to 'celebrate' their twentieth anniversary. She made plans for them to travel overseas, according to her husband's demands.

"During this journey, she happened into a curio shop much like the one in this building. She found the owner of the shop in a distressed state of mind and came to learn that his wife had recently died. She apologized for troubling him in his time of grief and offered her condolences. She asked him if he had any unusual antiques in his shop.

"The shopkeeper's countenance immediately changed and he looked at her with new interest as he presented her with a most unusual antique box. This box was said to have great powers.

"I guess that would be you?" Walt asked, wondering what kind of yarn the box was trying to spin.

"Please allow me to go on… Your mother was intrigued with the design and the craftsmanship of the wooden container that had been

built for it, but she could not help wondering what the wooden box might hold.

"She insisted that she could not buy 'a pig in a poke' and told the shopkeeper that he must open the box and show her what was inside before she could consider buying it.

"He asked her if she would agree that the wooden box itself was indeed worth a good amount if even to empty the contents and use it for storage of other items. She agreed that it was made from a very fine material and would be an attractive box for storage.

"When she asked the shopkeeper how much he was asking for it, he smiled and told her he would make her an incredible deal if only she promised never to listen to the voices inside her head.

"After considering this strange request for a little while, she finally agreed to the condition. She would definitely not listen to any voices in her head. Then, she paid the man the equivalent of twenty-five dollars for the box.

"When she had returned home from the vacation, she quickly unpacked her new antique treasure. She was delighted that the wooden box contained another box. A box with the likeness of a king's face carved into it, an incredible gold and silver crown serving as the lid.

"I knew this was about you. Everything is always about you, isn't it?" Walt was getting annoyed with this long tale that seemed to be nothing more than a fairy tale.

"Kindly allow me to finish, Walt. Her husband concluded that your mother had come upon quite a find. He thought it must be worth quite a bit with all of its gold and silver embellishments. He insisted that she sell it immediately. He wanted to use the money for a down payment on a new automobile. She ignored his request and refused to sell her new treasure, claiming that its value would surely increase over time.

"She was very pleased with the box and put it in a prominent place on her table. Each day she would look at it, wondering how much it might be worth.

"Finally, after several days, I spoke to her. I told your mother that she appeared to be very downhearted and asked her to tell me about herself. She revealed her deepest feelings.

"She said that she felt as though she were a prisoner with no chance of escape. She could not imagine being able to support herself if she left the man who was holding her captive, but she longed to be free.

"She told me that she dreamt of having a shop of her own, one where people would love to visit and buy exotic things like the one where she found the box. That was when I let her know that her dreams could come true if only she were willing to help me. To do for me what I needed to be done.

"Wait a minute! You got my mother involved in this?" Walt was distressed that his mother had kept this secret all those years, but even more upset that the box had coerced his mother to get involved in murder. His resolve to destroy the box grew stronger.

"Please, Walt. There is more you need to know. Your mother grew excited about my promise and, after a night of planning and while her husband was out drinking with his friends, she brought a military man home. His spirit became mine.

"Of course, I fulfilled her desire and, days later, she announced to her husband that she had bought a shop on the other side of town, one with an apartment above it where they could live. He became enraged that she had done this without involving him, asking where she had gotten the means to do so, and proceeded to beat her for what seemed like hours. When it was over, he sat down next to the table where the box was kept.

"By now her face was bloodied and bruised, as were her arms and legs. She had been pushed to the limits of sanity and could not face another moment of living with this man, this monster who could treat her like this after all of the years she had devoted to him.

"Quietly she crept across the room and removed the lid from this box and stepped back. With a sigh and two words, she freed herself

from him forever. 'Kill him,' she said and it was done. Her husband lay on the floor in shattered pieces.

"You gotta be shittin' me!" said Walt. "She killed my father?"

"The truth is that the man was not your father. You see, afterward, when I asked how I should reward her, her reply was 'a son,' and she described him in detail. He would be 20 years old and very intelligent, not too tall and not too good-looking. He would be compassionate, but firm and independent in his life, but would know nothing of how he had come to be. And so you were created."

"No, this is bullshit! You are my father? *You* are a spirit sucking box, there is no *way* that I'm just some result of a granted wish!" He stopped.

"Walt, I may be as close as you will get to the concept of father, but in the natural world, you truly have none."

"But you said I was twenty years old when she wished for me and I was... created? But I remember my childhood... I remember learning to ride a bike for the first time, going to the beach, elementary school, graduating high school, and all the rest of it."

"Your memories go only as far as your mother described them to you and you learned those things very well, making them a part of who you are. You say you remember these things you mention, but do you remember the details?

"Where did you live before coming here? What color was the bicycle you learned to ride? What was the name of the high school where you graduated? You have no idea, do you? Just as you have no memories of your father except what you were told of him, and memories of photographs. He was not what you were told, and now you know the truth."

Walt was beyond overwhelmed. He sank down in his chair and tried to remember everything he could about his childhood, but there was not much there. He couldn't remember faces of friends, playing with toys, visits to the playground, any actual details of his high school graduation, or anything about his younger years.

He couldn't remember anything that his mother hadn't described to him. But if he had never been to school *how could he read and write?*

"She taught you everything you know," the box answered his thought. *"All you are is what she made you to be, and nothing more."*

Walt suddenly had the urge to vomit. He rushed to the sink and began to heave from deep within his gut, but there was nothing there to throw up. Turning on the faucet, he took a drink of cold water. He wiped the sweat from his forehead, and turned to the box.

"So if I was never born, I can't die then, right? How 'bout I jump off the roof of the building to test that theory?"

"If you try it, you will simply cease to exist. That would be a waste of all you have become. You can live forever by my side and rule this world with me. Why would you waste that opportunity? You will have anything and everything you desire."

"Maybe that *is* true, but just like the desires that you have fulfilled for me, wouldn't it all be bullshit that goes wrong in the end? What good is that?"

"It only goes wrong because of your special situation. When I am complete and reborn, I can repair what is wrong and it will be as it should be. You must trust me."

"Trust you, right! Why should I trust you after what you did to Kathie?"

"It is your destiny, Walt. I created you for this moment."

Thirty-eight

John had been sitting across from the antique shop for about an hour in his car. From there he could watch the front of the building and he had a clear view of the alley. He had brought his camera just in case he could get some shots of Walt to use when interviewing people about his connection to the missing people.

He saw movement in the apartment and Walt came out and sat at the top of the stairs long enough to get a couple of clear shots of his face. John sat the camera on the seat next to him and drove to the nearest drug store where there was still one of those self-serve photo printers. He went inside and inserted his memory card and print out some 8x10 shots. He went to the cooler and grabbed a soda from the shelf, paid for everything and left.

It was about half past five when he got back to the office and he began to put his case together. He needed to know how it all fit before he either interviewed or arrested Walt. He could bring Walt in for questioning on an open charge and hold him for up to seventy-two hours. He wanted to be sure that when he finally made the arrest, the charges would stick.

He laid the file on his desk and arranged the photos in a line. He was almost certain that there was no connection between Walt and the death of Todd and Sara, except for his connection to Rachel who was now missing. He walked over to the copier and made copies of their photos and the police report and then placed them in a separate folder. Todd and Sara's case needed to stand on its own, and right now, he wasn't sure if any of it was related.

John took a good hard look at the rest of the photos. The witness statements seemed to indicate that they had all, at one time or other, been at the diner with Walt. The diner was in very close proximity to Walt's apartment.

The only thing missing was some kind of motive. Nothing had been said during any of his conversations about any arguments, problems or issues that may have existed between Walt and any of the missing. The only thing left to do now was to go to the apartment and talk to Walt. He would do that tomorrow.

Thirty-nine

Reality was crashing in on Walt as he realized the truth. He had racked his brain to come up with some evidence to disprove what the box had told him, but couldn't think of one thing. There was never any blood test or x-ray to point to the fact that he was human. He could not remember ever seeing a doctor since he had never been sick.

"So if I die, or as you say 'cease to exist,' I won't go to heaven or hell since I don't have a soul?" Walt asked.

"I am not aware that either exist. If you were to die, Walt, you will not BE anymore. This I do know."

Walt felt a chill of terror creep up his back. To know that there will be nothing after death was both frightening and liberating. If he couldn't go to hell, it didn't matter what he did, did it?

If he did as the box asked, he could live forever and never have to find out if what he was being told was true. In a way it would be like heaven without the whole death thing.

"So for you to be 'reborn,' you need a newborn human child. That will be the end of the way things are and we will both be powerful like gods? Is that what you're telling me?"

"Yes Walt, this is so."

"Fuck it all then. What do I need to do to get a newborn child?"

Of course, the box had a plan. Near the end of visiting hours, Walt would go to the hospital with a gym bag large enough to hold a child. He would enter through a service entrance and find the room where orderlies could change and shower between shifts.

He was to put on one of the green uniform shirts, take the bag to the floor where the newborns were kept, leave the bag in the hallway, walk right into the nursery, carry out a sleeping baby, put the baby in the bag and get out of there and drive home as fast as he could.

It sounded so easy the way the box explained it. But Walt wondered when was this supposed to happen?

"Tonight, it must be tonight," said the box, again answering his thoughts.

"Right, tonight, I'm in. Let's get this over with before I change my mind and just cause myself to cease to exist."

"It is a good decision, Walt." If the box could smile, it would have.

Walt hadn't driven a car for years, but Kathie's car was well maintained and the – if a non-human use the word – instinct for driving came back to him quickly. He drove the eight or ten miles to the hospital very carefully to avoid suspicion, travelling no faster than the speed limit on every street that he navigated.

He reached down to feel the gun behind his back. He hadn't carried the pistol since the altercation with the punk that day on his way home from work. The day that had started all of this crazy shit in motion.

Tucked securely in the elastic waistband of his underwear, it hurt like hell. *Stupid!* In the movies, they don't tuck the gun into the back of their jeans until they get out of the car. At the next red traffic light he struggled with his seatbelt and the gun, trying to work it free so he could just lay it on the seat until he got to where he was going.

It seemed to be hung up on his belt... just then he saw a cop car sitting at the same light, right across from him. He froze when out of nowhere the flashing lights began to glare like bolts of lightning into the night, blinding him with their first sweep. He was paralyzed with fear as the police car surged forward, siren blaring, blasting past him toward some emergency further behind him, down the street.

"Shit, Shit, Shit!" he yelled out loud still struggling with the grip of the gun, not realizing his finger was jammed against the trigger and the safety was off. BLAM! The gun went off, blowing out the back of his pants. The bullet went straight through the seat, plowing through the backseat and into the trunk.

"Fuck!" The gun pulled free of his belt and he whipped his arm forward. As he lost his grip, it slammed into the windshield causing a crack from the center of the glass to spread out, vertically, in front of him.

The bullet had not penetrated his skin anywhere, but it cleanly blew a hole in the back of his pants. The blowback, however, hurt like hell, and there were some powder burns on his ass. The windows were gone, shattered by the enclosed report of the handgun, which had wiped out his hearing. The unrelenting ringing in his ears now muffled the haze of the sounds of the street around him.

His head cleared and he realized the car behind him was blowing its horn. It was loud, but seemed far away. The light had changed to green and he was at a standstill trying to decide exactly what had just happened. He stepped on the gas and surged forward through the light turning into the first business entrance he came to.

In the parking lot of a convenience store, Walt came to a stop in a space as far from the door as possible and switched off the headlights. He jumped out of the car, slapping his smoldering ass and looking around for any witnesses. When he was satisfied that no one was watching, he tried to twist his head around to survey the damage to his pants.

He looked at the hole in the back of the car seat where a small wisp of smoke was trailing from it. He remembered what Mother had said about never lending your car or other possessions to someone else because they wouldn't take care of them like they did their own things. Damn if she wasn't right!

He felt a twinge of sorrow that spread like a triple shot of whiskey, not in the same warm and happy way, but just as powerful and overwhelming. In a moment he felt the grief in every part of his body. It was an ache that he would not be able to shake off.

The wisp of smoke coming from the car seat was not dying off, and he needed to do something. He turned around and looked for something to pour on the red glow that was spreading throughout the foam. He walked straight across the parking lot and grabbed the handle of the window-washing wand that was hanging near the gas pump, pushed it deep into the water and ran, dripping, for the smoking car seat.

He thrust the sponge side into the seat, swabbing it around inside the growing hole in the seat foam, but it was still burning. Again, he ran back to the reservoir, thrust the window cleaner into it, and ran back to the car.

Forty

John was sitting on his sofa flipping through the television channels with his remote control. He was mired in the strange clues marking his current caseload. He had the overwhelming feeling that he was very close to solving it, and that something could break at any moment and blow things wide open. A relaxing night of mindless occupation in front of the television was out of the question.

He might as well go and check out this Walt guy's house. Yeah, maybe he could see something that he could use to nail the bastard to the wall. He got dressed, strapped on his gun, grabbed his camera and his badge, and headed for the door.

He didn't want to attract any attention if he was seen along the street, so he was wearing blue jeans tonight. He pulled up almost across the street from the antique shop. There were no lights on, and it appeared that Walt was not at home. He would hang out at least until he felt sleepy. After all, he was not officially on the clock, and this was not official surveillance, just something he needed to do.

Meanwhile, Walt had arrived at the hospital. He parked the car along the curb in the shadows between two streetlights. Getting out, he tucked the gun into the back of his pants again, and walked around the building to look for an unlocked door.

As he turned a corner, he saw a maintenance man slowly pushing a cart full of trash toward a dumpster. The man had wedged a doorstop in the door to get back in easily without using the keys. Walt noticed that the man must have left the keys inside because the key holder clipped to his belt was empty. He took advantage of the opportunity, slipping through the door, and pulling the wedge out allowing it to close and lock behind him.

It would take a few minutes for the maintenance man to empty the cart before he tried to get back into the building and discover that he was locked out. He would have to walk all the way to the front of the building to get back in.

Walt found himself at the end of a hall on the ground floor. To one side of the hall was a room. Pushing the door open, Walt saw that he was in a men's dressing room complete with lockers and several of them were carelessly unlocked. *Maybe this is going to be easier than I thought,* Walt hoped.

He opened the first locker and it was empty except for a bag of trash from a burger joint. He tried the next locker and hit pay dirt. Hanging in the locker was a uniform that might belong to an orderly, and better than that, it looked like it had already been worn through a shift and had a few stains on it that would give it an air of authenticity.

He decided that the scrubs were large enough to wear right over his clothes and started to put them on when he noticed the bloodstain on the front. It was about the size of his closed fist and still slightly moist.

Walt considered for a moment whether it would present a problem going to the maternity ward with blood on his shirt. Since there was no time to look for something else, he slipped it on over his head. "Fuck it" he said to himself.

He put his shoes back on and headed to the door and the hall outside. As he stuck his head through the door to make sure no one saw him leaving, he heard keys rattling outside the building and muffled cursing. *Damn! The maintenance man had his keys with him!*

Walt broke into a sprint down the hall, turned the corner and the service elevator was right there in front of him. It seemed it was just waiting, open and welcoming, for a passenger. He pushed the button for the maternity ward floor and the doors closed.

The elevator made a bell tone when it reached the floor and the doors slid open. Since it was a bit past visiting hours, the halls were pretty empty and he slid past the nurse's station and followed the signs, with blue and pink bears and bunnies on them, to the nursery.

As he walked slowly past the large window, he looked inside the room where the babies were kept. He saw two nurses checking the charts of the babies and doing their first round of the night.

Some of the tiny beds were empty. Some of the babies must be in the rooms with their mothers, he thought. He walked back down the hall, and looked into rooms as he went, looking for a mother with a baby.

The first one he saw was holding her baby. She had been trying to breastfeed and had dozed off for a second. There was no allowance for hesitation in this plan. He slithered through the door and over to the side of the bed, eased the baby from its mother's grip and turned to leave the room.

As he looked up he was standing face to face with the floor nurse, who aside from being a rather large woman, was standing looking at him with her mouth hanging open, paralyzed with surprise.

A moment of her hesitation was all Walt needed. He pushed past her and ran down the hall to the elevator. He struggled to get a good grip on the baby as he reached for the button to summon the elevator. There was no time to wait, he ran for the door marked stairs and plunged through it holding the baby to his chest.

It seemed like it only took moments to descend the four flights of stairs and he burst through the door of the first floor. Down the hall he ran and out through the same door he had entered the building through. Again the janitor had propped it open and as it slammed shut, the doorstop failed to keep it from closing.

He ran to his car, grabbing for the keys in his pocket, but he was having trouble reaching inside of the scrubs for the pocket of his jeans. As he reached the car he took hold of the door handle and found it was unlocked. He threw it open and laid the baby, miraculously still asleep, on the passenger's seat. He stuffed some towels from the floor around it to keep it from rolling off the seat, and shut the door.

He ran around the car to the driver's side and tore the shirt and pants of the scrubs off and threw them on the ground. Then he grabbed the keys from his pocket, the gun from the back of his pants and jumped in the car. He threw the gun onto the seat next to the baby, and shoved the key in the ignition and turned it. The tired old car roared to life.

John was still parked in front of Walt's apartment and growing more and more tired of waiting for something, anything, to happen. It seemed as though Walt was not coming home any time soon, and it was time for some covert action. He grabbed his gun, police radio and badge off the seat and hopped out of the car.

He walked across the street and stood in the doorway of the abandoned antique shop. The streetlight fell just so, covering him in shadow. He pulled a small box from his pocket and opened it. From the neatly displayed collection he could see the triangular shaped lock pick shining there even in the dim light. He picked it out quickly and pushed it into the lock, jiggling it into place until he heard a click and the doorknob turned.

John pushed the door open just far enough to get through it and closed it quietly behind him. He turned looking into the light filtering through the window coverings. He pulled a small flashlight from his pocket and turned it on. It seemed kind of smoky for some reason and the beam of his flashlight was muddled in haze and floating dust particles.

He noticed a metallic taste in his mouth. It was vaguely familiar, but as John sniffed the air there seemed to be nothing that smelled unusual. He scanned the front room and off to one side and saw the door to the stairwell.

He walked over to the door and tried it. It was unlocked. He decided to check out the second floor if there was time after he cleared this floor. Just then he heard a car pull up and the engine shut off. He turned his small light into a dark corner away from the windows.

He heard a muffled voice like someone was having a conversation inside of the car but he could only make out one voice. When the car door was opened, the conversation was louder but still muffled. It appeared to be a one-sided conversation because he could still only hear one voice.

The car door slammed shut and someone was climbing the stairs on the side of the building. The door to the apartment above opened and closed.

Forty-one

"Shhh little baby, everything will be ok," said Walt as he picked his pistol up off the seat and tucked it into the back of his pants. He wrapped the baby in one of the towels from the seat and lifted it out of the car. Stepping back, he kicked the door closed with his foot. "Now all we have to do is introduce you to this friend of mine, and we can all relax for a while."

The baby whimpered a bit and Walt bounced it in his arms. "Come on now, little one. This is no time to be crying. You're going to be the most powerful person in the world and powerful people don't cry like little babies." He climbed the steps to the landing and balanced the baby in one hand while he unlocked the door with the other. He closed the door and locked it behind him.

"Hey, Mr. Spirit Box! I did what you asked and got the baby just like you said." He laid the pistol on one of the end tables and the infant on the sofa. Walking over to the table where the box was sitting, Walt asked, "So what's next? What do I need to do to finish this?"

"Walt, you must prepare the child now. Remove his clothes and wash him, then he will be ready for my acceptance."

"What? I have to give him a bath first? I've never bathed a kid before. What if I drop him? What if he drowns?"

"No Walt. You will not prepare a bath. You must be simply clean the infant with warmed water. Use a cloth and wipe his skin gently. Immersion is not necessary. He must be purified for my entry into the body."

Walt walked to the bathroom grumbling under his breath. He turned the faucet to warm and let it run while he fetched a clean washcloth out of the cabinet. When the water was just warm, he moistened the washcloth.

Coming back into the living room, Walt groused, "So do I have to wash the whole thing, or just the face?"

"It is but a small task. Simply cleanse the face and body of impurities, and that will be the end of it. The preparation will be complete."

"Right," Walt said as he removed the towel from the baby. The nightgown and cap provided by the hospital were easily removed from the tiny baby. Walt took more time taking off the baby's diaper. He didn't want to be surprised by a messy diaper just now. He only wanted to be sure to do everything exactly right. After all, he did *not* want to have to go through all of this again.

"Oh shit!"

John was sure he had heard someone say "Oh shit" as he moved toward the door. He could see now that this door led to a stairwell and assumed that the stairwell connected the shop to the apartment above.

As he moved carefully through the shop, he was so focused on getting to the door that he neglected to watch his step. Before he knew what was happening, he tripped and fell face forward on top of something that went *crunch*! With great effort he suppressed his urge to cry out.

The taste of metal was stronger now for some reason and he reached for the flashlight he had dropped as he landed. *It was dried blood!* He thought as he recognized that metallic taste in his mouth. With that, his mind came to the grips with the fact that he was laying in a pile of partially crushed, dried corpses. He muffled a yelp as he quickly got on his feet.

As he shone the flashlight down at the floor, he counted three or four corpses. It was difficult to tell because there were various loose body parts and one of the corpses was headless. Half of one of the bodies had been crushed as he had fallen on it.

Upstairs Walt thought he heard a noise coming from the shop downstairs, but he was determined to take care of the business at hand before checking it out.

"Have you injured the boy, Walt?"

"What?"

"You said 'Oh shit?' "

"Uh…well, I fucked up. It isn't a boy, it's a girl!"

The baby was puckering up its tiny face, getting ready to cry, as a red glow began to flood the room.

The box spoke in outrage, *"A girl? This cannot be so, I told you to bring me a male infant child, not a female!"*

"Now wait just a second, motherfucker! You did NOT say it had to be a boy! All this time, you said infant child, infant child, and never once did you say 'male infant child!' You didn't say it had to be a boy… AND you have no idea how fucking hard it was to steal this kid!" The baby's arms and legs were flailing as it lay uncovered, yet still no cries could be heard.

"This is not acceptable, I cannot spend the rest of eternity in the body of a female. Surely you must have realized this. You must return and bring a male child!"

"Excuse me?" Walt folded the towel back across the baby and stood up to confront the box. "I will not go back to that hospital. I am sure the police are looking for me by now. We have to do this right now with this girl or you and me are both screwed!"

John could hear yelling now, but he could not tell what was being said. There was no way to tell how many people were in that apartment upstairs, and he wasn't prepared to run into a shit storm of maniacs...

He pulled his police radio from his pocket and turned it on, careful to not turn it up too loud. It was time to call this in and get some backup. The yelling continued upstairs.

John's heart was pounding as he put the radio up to his mouth and spoke quietly, trying not to sound panicked. "This is detective Hazard requesting backup at the antique shop on..." he hesitated. He could not remember the name of the street he was on.

"Which antique shop? We have two listed here," came the voice from the radio.

"The antique shop that is out of business! The one with the apartment above it!" John replied frantically.

"I know the one you're talking about, hang on..." silence from the radio, then..."I have a car in the area, E.T.A. in five minutes."

"Suspect or suspects are presumed armed. I need the coroner. I have four bodies. I'm not sure what I am facing here."

"Copy that detective, proceed with caution."

He switched off the radio.

Forty-two

"Did you hear that?" asked Walt, "I thought I heard someone talking downstairs."

"We are out of time. Bring the child," said the box, *"lay it on the table next to me, and stand back."*

Walt did as he was told. He pushed the box further back on the table and removed the lid. Then he walked to the sofa, picked up the naked little girl in the towel and carried her over to the table. That was when she started to cry. She cried like her life depended on it, and it did.

"What the fuck?" John said out loud, pointing the flashlight in the direction of the door to the stairwell where the sound seemed to come from. He thought to himself, *Was that a baby? It couldn't be a baby. Could it?*

The baby wailed even louder. Now he knew there was no waiting for backup. He had to do something and do it now. He rushed to the door and turned the knob and pushed, slamming his shoulder into the door. It was locked. He stepped back and kicked the door next to the doorknob.

It made a loud noise, but the door didn't budge. He decided to break the glass panel in the door and reach through to unlock it. He looked around for something to use to break the glass. Lying on a shelf next to him was a metal statuette of three monkeys, the 'see no evil, hear no evil, speak no evil' trio. He took hold of it and smashed it against the glass, which shattered, but could not be removed because it was embedded with wire.

Now he began to panic. Surely whoever was up there knew he was there. Frantically he pounded against the glass again and again until he had broken through enough space in the wire to put his arm through and unlock the door. He charged up the stairs, his firearm held out in front of him.

Walt had heard the bang on the door in the shop below.

"Somebody is downstairs and it sounds like they're trying to break down the door. You better hurry the fuck up!" He picked up his pistol and chambered a round.

The box began to glow blue and then a kind of blue-green. The light was growing brighter, and Walt could hear a kind of humming sound as the table began to vibrate. The baby on the table was quiet now, and Walt tried to turn away in horror as her mouth began to open, wider, then wider still. He listened for the now familiar sound of her jawbone shattering, but the tiny baby bones were soft and did not shatter.

He heard the crash of breaking glass and pounding downstairs, but the humming sound in the room was getting louder and louder. This was not the phenomenon of the spirit extraction he had seen before.

Suddenly, the ceiling above the box seemed to turn to melt away, rolling and swirling above him. Flashing lights came from the center of the growing vortex, and a bolt of lightning shot into the ceiling. Something was rising from the opening of the box. The baby on the table was shaking and her back was arched as she began to rise into the air.

The tangled mass coming up from the box began to unravel. Faces began to appear, the faces of young, old, men, women, and children. The mass of faces was growing larger by the second, and Walt could see the expressions of terror on each one as it peeled away from the rest.

Suddenly from the hundreds of faces swirling in front of him, Walt saw the face of Greg. The faces of the others were frozen in terror, but Greg was looking right at him. And was he…smiling?

The specter of Greg moved toward Walt and opened its mouth to say in a loud ghostly whisper, "Your turn." As the words left Greg's spirit lips, John Hazard burst through the door.

Walt hesitated for just a moment before raising his pistol toward the detective. That gave John an opportunity to get off the first shot, and then a second, hitting Walt first in the shoulder spinning him halfway around, and then in the right temple, knocking him to the floor.

At first John wasn't sure exactly what the fuck was happening, there was shit swirling on the ceiling, faces and bodies of all kinds of people flying about the room, and a naked baby hanging in the air halfway to the ceiling with a giant mouth gaping open.

There was no time to freak out. John knew he had to act. Stepping forward, he put his foot on Walt's neck and put another bullet into his forehead just to be sure that he wouldn't get up again. Then he holstered his weapon and moved into action to save the baby.

By now, the baby had risen closer to the swirling vortex that used to be Walt's ceiling. He tried reaching up to grab her but couldn't reach her from the floor. He stepped up on a chair and put his hands around her, but lost his balance as the chair tipped over beneath him. He expected to fall back to the floor, but instead, the baby remained suspended there and John was left holding onto the baby for dear life.

The baby's body was hard as stone and hanging from it did not even so much as cause it to dip. John weighed more than two hundred pounds these days, which should have been enough to let gravity do its work. He had to think of something else fast.

Since the baby was hovering about a foot below the swirling ceiling, John thought he might be able to swing his legs up and find a solid foothold somewhere on the ceiling to push them back down to the ground. He got a better grip on the baby and swung himself backward, then thrust his legs up toward where the ceiling should be. His feet should have made contact, but there was nothing solid there, and his legs fell back to hang below him.

John felt the panic begin to build. He had to think of something. It was useless to be just hanging here, and he did not want to let the baby be sucked away. It was apparent that the source of the energy that was creating this anomaly was the box sitting on the table. The spirits swirling around him as he held on to the baby were flowing out from it.

Maybe he could destroy the box. Perhaps then he could save the baby and stop whatever was going on here. His first instinct was to smash it. He let go of the baby and dropped to the floor. He reached for the box and put both hands around it to lift it up. He could feel the vibration and it was cold as ice.

All he had to do was smash it on the floor. He tried to lift it, but it would not budge. It was if it was attached to the table and, no matter how hard he pulled, neither the box nor the table would budge.

He let go of the box and put his hands under the edge of the table, lifting up to flip it over. As small as the table was, he could not move it. He pulled with everything he had and then got down in a squat and tried pushing up, but still nothing happened.

There seemed to be no end of the spirits flowing out of the box, and now the ceiling was pulsating. It was a roiling, giant whirlpool of blue and green light and a loud shrill sound filled the room, like the sound of the screaming wind of a hurricane.

He had to stop whatever was happening. He stepped back from the table while reaching for his pistol aiming it at the box. Two shots ricocheted away, one into the wall and one buried itself in the door of the refrigerator. "This fucking thing is indestructible!" He shouted in frustration.

"The box is indestructible as long as the spirit of the king remains inside it." He was startled by the woman's voice that sounded close to his right ear. He spun around quickly and came face to face with one of the spirits hovering there. A face that was somehow familiar to him, the face of a beautiful woman.

"What?!?"

"Soon you will see, when the king is free, then the box can be destroyed. There will only be a moment to act before the power is transferred to the child, so you must act quickly. The moment is near."

It was the face of Rachel, the woman he had been searching for, the girl in the photo, the one who murdered Todd and his girlfriend. As quickly as she had appeared, she was gone again into the swirling mass above his head.

He had only seconds to decide on a course of action, so he aimed his gun and braced his arm with his free hand. There would be only one chance, one shot, and he was shaking badly from the shock of what he was witnessing.

The screeching sound began to lower in pitch, and when it settled into a low thrum, a large spirit burst from the box. Its face exactly matched the one carved into the side of the box. This must be the moment. This was the king and this was the shot. John squeezed the trigger… and missed! The bullet slammed into the wall shattering the plaster and raising a small cloud of dust.

The box was still glowing as John steadied his aim. The spirit of the king lunged at him, knocking him off balance. As the glowing form passed through him, it was as if his stomach had been pressed in a vise, and vomit spewed from his mouth like an open valve on a fire hose.

He felt himself falling to the floor and, in desperation, he fired his next shot. The bullet was true to the target and hit the glowing box. John fell to the floor with the last of his stomach contents flying out in front of him and he landed there in his own vomit.

The box had exploded into a cloud of sparks as it was struck, and blue plasma and shards of broken pottery flew in all directions striking the walls of the room with incredible force. The swirling mass near the ceiling turned from a blue green color to bright red, and a blinding flash of lightning emitted and streaked about the room. Suddenly the entire area of the vortex blew clean through the ceiling and the roof above it with a loud "Boom."

"NOOOOOOOOOOO!" The spirits screamed out as they began to fly through the roof and up into the night sky. John managed to turn himself over and he lay on the floor helplessly watching in a state of shock.

Suddenly the baby dropped from mid-air, landing on top of him. He tried to catch it but his arms were slippery with vomit and the baby slid to the floor beside him. As the flashes of light and the glowing faded, and the last spirits flew from the box, John saw that the baby was conscious and breathing and seemed virtually unharmed.

He tried to stand straining to get his footing, but something slammed into the back of his head. Around him the pieces of the broken chair fell to the floor. He turned and saw the spirit of the king floating just above the floor behind him. He tried again to stand in order to face the king. As he struggled to get up, he heard voices outside the door yelling "Police." John's backup had finally arrived.

Forty-three

The patrol car turned the corner onto the street as directed by the dispatcher. John Hazard was known for being a bit strange, and the two officers occupying the car had grimaced when his name was mentioned during the call for backup. But an emergency involving three or four bodies and an incident in progress was all that mattered.

Dispatch had no communication with Hazard since the call came in, so for all they knew they could be walking into a shitstorm of bullets and blood, maybe even an officer down. John could already be dead.

A couple of blocks back, the siren had been turned off to avoid warning the perpetrators of their arrival, but they continued to use the flashing lights to avoid collisions with any cars that may be out and about in the area.

As bright as the flashing lights on the car were, they seemed dim in comparison to the blue-green light coming from the apartment above the antique shop. As they skidded to a stop in front of the building, they heard gunshots coming from inside the upstairs apartment.

One of the officers, the passenger, communicated their arrival to headquarters through the microphone clipped to his shoulder as he stepped out of the car. "Officers on the scene, shots fired…"

The driver grabbed the shotgun from the console and joined the officer on the other side of the car facing the building. There was a sound of an explosion just then and they both dove to the ground. They waited there for a moment while bits of gravel, boards, plaster and chunks of roof began to rain down on them.

They jumped to their feet and ran for the stairs. As they looked up, watching the door for any movement, they saw a blue light shooting into the sky and shining streaks of what looked like, as impossible as it seemed, people flying up into the sky.

Continuing to watch as they climbed to the top of the landing, they heard a crash from inside the apartment. The bright light that had been streaming out from the windows began to fade. The officers looked at each other and, without a sound, readied their weapons. In position now, one of the officers yelled, "Police!" as the other plunged forward and crashed through the door.

Just inside of that apartment, they froze in their tracks. To one side, there was a body lying on the floor, bullet holes to the head and torso. To the other side, was a bloodied John Hazard half lying, half sitting on the floor with a baby in his arms and broken pieces of a chair scattered around him.

"Police! Freeze, or I'll shoot," yelled the first officer in the door. Behind John was a huge bearded man, better described as a glowing ghost-like translucent creature. His brain finally registered that this was no ordinary suspect. The pattern of the wallpaper behind could be seen behind the spirit, as they looked right through him.

The entire ceiling of the room had been blown out, and they could see the night sky above them as they held their weapons on the ghostly figure that appeared fixated, looking upward at the stars. One officer circled around the bearded spirit while the other lowered his weapon and moved forward to assist John and the baby.

As he reached to take hold of John's hand, a strong wind began to blow through the room and the large ghost seemed to turn to sand and blow away. John and the officers stared up at the gaping hole in the ceiling. All could say with certainty that they had never witnessed a stranger sight until the body on the floor, most of the furniture, appliances, dishes and other various knick-knacks began turning to sand in the same fashion and blowing away without a sound.

The officers had been in the apartment for less than a minute and now, for the most part, it was empty except for the baby and the detective, and each other. As they looked around the empty room, they said, almost in unison, "What the fuck just happened?"

John looked from one to the other, and said, "I have no idea what the hell that was, but we need to come up with a really good story before we file the report. If we write this up like we saw it, we are all headed for a nice long vacation in a mental institution..."

Forty-four

John handed the baby to one of the officers who wrapped it snug in the towel and held it close. It made no sound, but appeared to have survived the ordeal without any marks. All three adults were in a state of shock from what they had just experienced.

John was the first to speak now. "I can't write this report the way things went down. You guys probably figured out that I did not follow proper procedure, and then who the hell would believe any of this?"

"I think we can all agree on that," replied the officer holding the baby. "I don't think we can even let anyone see this crime scene. I have no idea how to explain it!"

"What if the crime scene wasn't here? Then we wouldn't have to explain anything, just write it up like a regular crime scene report," said the other officer.

"What do you mean, if it wasn't here?" asked John.

The officer pulled a lighter from his pocket and flicked it on to a long flame, and put it out again. "This is what I mean," he smiled. He walked over to the gas range and started turning knobs. He looked at his partner and said, "Get the baby out of here. I got this covered."

John and the other officer went out the door with the baby and down the stairs. As they reached the patrol car in the front of the building, they turned to see the other officer exiting the front door of the antique shop. He closed the door behind him and ran to the car.

"I started a couple of small fires inside the shop. There were bodies in there that already appeared to be burned or something. Did you see what happened to them, Hazard?"

"No, they were laying there when I went through the shop earlier, but they're related somehow," John said. "I'll explain it all to you guys after we take care of this."

"Oh, it's already taken care of," replied the officer. "Keep watching."

As they stood by the car, they could see the glow of the flames coming from inside the antique shop. The light began to grow in intensity as the flames spread.

"Uh, fellas, I think we should move the car," he said. "This is gonna be big."

Hazard got in the back while the two officers sat in the front seat with the baby. They drove about a half block away and watched the fire grow. After several minutes, the flames had spread and most of the lower half of the building was fully involved. "Shouldn't we call the fire department?" John asked.

"Not until…" *Wharoom!* A loud explosion interrupted the officer's response and debris began to rain down on the block surrounding the building "…now." He finished his sentence and grabbed his radio microphone.

"This is Officer Bradley. We're here at the scene with Detective Hazard. We need the fire department and an ambulance immediately.

"There's been a couple of explosions and we have a burning building fully involved. We also have an infant that needs transport to the hospital."

As he finished the call, he put his hands up to his head and leaned back against the car seat. John spoke up, "Isn't this some shit? After we hand this over to the emergency crew, you can follow me to the coffee shop down the road so we can sort this story out for our reports."

An hour later, the coffee shop was pretty empty with the exception of a few customers who had strayed in after last call at the local bar. The three men sitting in the corner booth were grateful for the noise and laughter coming from the drunks because it prevented anyone from overhearing them.

Forty-five

John sat at his desk reading over his report. It was the best story he had ever come up with during his entire career. Everything was all buttoned up nice and neat. In fact, it was so good he was concerned that it might seem suspicious to the chief when he read it.

In one night, he had closed a murder case, four missing persons cases and a child abduction. He'd prevented another possible murder and, who knows, maybe even saved the planet. The saving the planet part would *not* be making it into the report.

For now, all he could think of was getting a good long sleep and, as he laid the folder with the report on the chief's desk, he muttered to himself, "I *definitely* need a vacation!"

Later that morning, the chief sat reading the report. "Hazard," was all he said as he shook his head.

After investigating the murder and the missing persons cases over the past couple of weeks, there was a clear correlation to the suspect, Walter Turner.

I was driving to the subject's home to begin surveillance when I was alerted that a baby had been abducted from the county hospital. I was informed that a man matching Turner's description was involved.

Upon arrival at the Turner residence, I witnessed the subject entering the building carrying the infant. Immediately I called for backup. I entered the building through the antique shop entrance on the lower floor of the building where I discovered the decomposing bodies of four adults. One of the bodies was the murder suspect I had been investigating. The others were the three missing people.

I then heard Mr. Turner yelling loudly and the child crying upstairs. I could smell smoke so I headed for the stairway leading up to Mr. Turner's apartment. By the time I ascended the stairs, the suspect, Mr. Walt Turner, had already set fire to the building.

I attempted to rescue the baby and struggled with the suspect. Mr. Turner drew a weapon and I was forced to return fire. The suspect fell to the floor and I picked up the baby.

At that point in time, backup arrived and I handed over the baby. Officer Tanger left the building with the baby, and I tried to assist Mr. Turner but he was deceased. Officer Bradley called for fire units, and an ambulance. As the flames approached the gas stove, I ran from the building to escape the impending explosion.

All four bodies of the adult victims and the suspect were incinerated in the fire and resulting explosion, as was any other evidence related to the case. No further investigation of this matter is warranted.

This case is closed.

About the Author

JH Glaze was born in Niles, Ohio and currently resides in Atlanta GA. This is his first novel in a series of stories starring Detective John Hazard.

He lives with his wife and editor, Susan Grimm, their dogs, Harley and Jake, and JoJo, the Senegal parrot.

This novel and the next in the series, 'NorthWest', were written almost entirely while riding the public transit system in Atlanta, (MARTA), during the commute to the "Day Job", and a portion was written while under the influence of Starbucks, and Caribou Coffee.

To find more information, search the web for Jeff Glaze ,JH Glaze, and MostCool Media.

The third novel in the series is currently in development and is called 'Send No Angel'

If you like this story, please tell your friends, extended family, co-workers, and complete strangers to read it.

If you would like to be a character in one of the stories written by JH Glaze, send your real name and a nickname for yourself to jeff@mostcoolmedia.com We will contact you if your name is to be used.

Thanks for reading and remember, *don't look in the box!*

Visit The Author's Site: www.JHGlaze.com

Made in the USA
San Bernardino, CA
06 May 2014